RAPE
A Love Story

RAPE

A Love Story

Joyce Carol Oates

ATLANTIC BOOKS
LONDON

First published in the United States in 2003 by Carroll
and Graf, an imprint of Avalon Publishing Group Inc.

First published in Great Britain in 2005 by Atlantic Books,
an imprint of Grove Atlantic Ltd.

1 3 5 7 9 8 6 4 2

A CIP catalogue record for this book is available
from the British Library.

1 84354 412 1

Printed and bound in Great Britain by
Mackays of Chatham plc, Chatham Kent

Atlantic Books
An imprint of Grove Atlantic Ltd
Ormond House
26–27 Boswell Street
London WC1N 3JZ

RAPE
A Love Story

Part I

She Had It Coming

AFTER SHE WAS GANG-RAPED, kicked and beaten and left to die on the floor of the filthy boathouse at Rocky Point Park. After she was dragged into the boathouse by the five drunken guys—unless there were six, or seven—and her twelve-year-old daughter with her screaming *Let us go! Don't hurt us! Please don't hurt us!* After she'd been chased by the guys like a pack of dogs jumping their prey, turning her ankle, losing both her high-heeled sandals on the path beside the lagoon. After she'd begged them to leave her daughter alone and they'd laughed at her. After she'd made the decision, Christ knows what she was thinking, to cross through Rocky Point Park instead of taking the longer way around, to home. To where she was living with her daughter in a rented row house on Ninth Street around the corner from her mother's brick house on Baltic Avenue. Ninth Street was lighted and populated even at this late hour. Rocky Point Park was mostly deserted at this late hour. Crossing the park along the lagoon, a scrubby overgrown path. Saving ten minutes, maybe. Thinking it would be nice to cross through the park, moonlight on the lagoon, no matter the lagoon is scummy and littered with beer cans, food wrappers, butts. Making that decision, a split second out of an entire life and the life is altered forever. Along the lagoon, past the old waterworks boarded up and covered in graffiti for years, and the boathouse that's been broken into, vandalized by kids. After she'd recognized their faces, might even have smiled at them, it's Fourth of July, fireworks at the Falls, firecrackers, car horns and whistles, the high school baseball game, festive atmosphere. Yes she might've smiled at them, and so she was asking for it. Might've been an edgy, nervous smile the way you'd smile at a snarling dog, still she smiled, that lipstick smile of Teena Maguire's, and that hair of hers. She had it coming, she was asking for it. Guys who'd been drifting around the park for hours looking for trouble. Looking for some fun. Drinking beer and tossing cans into the lagoon and all the firecrackers they had, they'd set off. Throwing firecrackers at cars, at dogs, at swans and geese and mallards on the lagoon sleeping with their heads neat-tucked beneath their wings, Christ! It's hilarious to see the water-fowl wake up fast and squawk like they're being killed and flap their wings like crazy flying away, even the fat ones. The All–Niagara Falls High School game went into extra innings, now the brightly lit baseball field was darkened, bleachers emptied, most of the crowd gone. Except these drifting packs of guys. The youngest just kids, the oldest in their late twenties. Neighborhood guys whose faces Teena Maguire would know, maybe not their given names but their family names, as the guys knew her, at least recognized her from the neighborhood though she was older than they were, calling out

Hey! Hey there! Mmmm, good-lookin'! Hey foxy lady, whereya goin'? After she'd smiled at them not slackening her pace. After she'd reached for her daughter's arm like her daughter was a small child and not twelve years old. *Show us how your titties bounce, foxy lady! Heyheyhey whereya goin'?* After she'd gotten herself trapped. After she'd teased them. Provoked them. Bad judgment. Must've been drinking. The way she was dressed. The way Teena Maguire often dressed. Summer nights, especially. Partying over on Depew Street. Party spilling out onto the street. Loud rock music. That kind of behavior, she had it coming. Where's her husband? Doesn't that woman have a husband? What the hell is she doing out alone with her twelve-year-old daughter, in Rocky Point Park at midnight? Endangering the safety of a minor? Endangering the morals of a minor? Look: Teena Maguire probably was having a few beers with the guys. Smoking dope with the guys. Maybe she was hinting at something she'd like to be paid for? In cash, or in dope. A woman like that, thirty-five years old and dressed like a teenager. Tank top, denim cutoffs, shaggy bleached-blond hair frizzed around her face. Bare legs, high-heeled sandals? Tight sexy clothes showing her breasts, her ass, what's she expect? Midnight of July Fourth, fireworks at the Falls ended at eleven. Still there's partying all over the city. How much beer has been consumed in Niagara Falls tonight by residents and visitors? Better believe it's a lot. Like, the volume of water rushing over the Horseshoe Falls in a minute! And there's Teena Maguire, drunk on her feet, witnesses would report. One of her boyfriends, guy named Casey over on Depew, a

5

keg party at his place spilling out into the backyard and street and neighbors complaining, wild weird bluegrass music Ricky Skaggs and Kentucky Thunder for hours. This Casey, he's a welder at Niagara Pipe. He's married and has four kids. Separated from his wife, must be Teena Maguire's doing. That woman! What kind of a mother would drag her young daughter with her to a drunken party and then on foot through Rocky Point Park at that hour, what kind of poor judgment, she's lucky it wasn't worse what happened to her, and what happened to the girl, couldn've been a lot worse if they'd been black men, coked-up niggers invading the park it would've been a hell of a lot worse, the woman had to be drunk, high on coke herself, partying since early evening and by midnight you can figure the state she was in, how the hell could Teena Maguire even recognize who had sex with her? And how many?

Some of the things that would be said of your mother Teena Maguire after she was gang-raped, kicked and beaten and left to die on the floor of the filthy boathouse at Rocky Point Park in the early minutes of July 5, 1996.

Rookie Cop, 1994

H<small>E WASN'T THAT YOUNG.</small> He didn't look young and he didn't act young and most of the time he didn't feel young. He was a rookie, though. A damn rookie almost thirty years old and just out of Police Academy.

Weird a guy like him wearing a uniform! He had not the temperament for wearing a uniform. He had not the temperament for following orders, saluting. He had not the temperament for listening closely to others, designated as superiors. (*His* superiors? Bullshit.) Since grade school he'd had trouble with authority. Restless under the eye of anybody and looking to find his own private way, sullen and sly like a chimp hiding something behind his back.

What he liked was the idea of justice, though. Putting-things-back-to-right he liked. Such abstractions as law, good conduct, valor in service, eye-for-an-eye, tooth-for-a-tooth.

The U.S. flag had a powerful effect on him sometimes. Not if the damn thing hung down limp but if there was a wind, not too strong a wind but a decent wind, making the red-white-blue cloth ripple, shimmer in the sun.

Saluting that flag, he'd feel tears come into his eyes.

Also, he liked guns.

Now he was a cop and wore a gun on his hip, holstered up, liking the familiar weight of it, like an extra appendage. And the eyes of strangers drifting onto it. With respect.

The police service revolver he was issued, like his badge and uniform, he liked, and other firearms he would acquire singly, as a collector. Nothing fancy, he had not that kind of money. A cop with his shrewd eyes open, he knew there was money, different sources of money, available, if not immediately, then someday. He would pursue these sources. In the meantime, his purchases were modest. He liked handguns, and he liked rifles. He had not (yet) much experience with a shotgun, so he could not speak for that. (No one in his family had been a hunter. They were city people: factory workers, dockside workers, truckers. Dublin in the 1930s, Buffalo/Lackawanna in the 1940s. He was mostly estranged from them now, and the hell with them.)

A gun excited him. It was a good feeling. Quickened his pulse so he could actually feel it. Sometimes, a tinge in the groin. What that meant, he had little curiosity about knowing. He was not a man to examine his own mind or motives. Frowning into a mirror, he saw what had to be done, and done deftly: brushing his teeth, shaving, dampening and combing his hair, practice-smiling to flash the idea of a smile but not to show his crazy-crooked left canine tooth. He was a man of little vanity, though. Asked the barber to shave his head at the back, sides, keep the rest trimmed short so it more resembled wires than human hair, glinting like something that might cut your fingers if you touched it.

It wasn't 100 percent true, he didn't feel young. A gun in his hand, he felt pretty good. Cleaning a gun. Loading a gun, aiming a gun. Firing a gun (at the firing range) and never flinching at the noise or the recoil. Noting calmly if you'd struck your target (heart, head) and if not, how far off you were. And try again.

The thing about guns: you were always improving. A matter of discipline, progress. In school he had always been uncertain of his standing, sometimes he did all right and his teachers praised him (such a tall snaky-lean kid with moody eyes and a close-shut unsmiling mouth, his nervous teachers were quick to praise him), other times he fucked up. Hit-or-miss it seemed. Books made him uneasy, resentful. Damn words, numerals. Like stones shoved into his mouth, too many and he'd choke.

But guns. A gun is different. The more you handle a gun, the more expert you become. And the gun gets comfortable with you, too.

His NFPD uniform wasn't his first. He'd enlisted in the U.S. Army out of high school. In the army they'd taught him to shoot. Almost he'd been selected for an elite sniper team. But he hadn't been that good, for those guys were really good, awesome. He'd conceded it was probably just as well.

Might've liked it too much. Killing.

They'd sent him to the Persian Gulf. Operation Desert Shield that became Operation Desert Storm. Only just a few years ago in his life but it seemed longer. In the life of his country, so fast-moving and not-looking-back, the Gulf War was nearly forgotten. He wasn't a man to look back, and he wasn't a man of regrets. What happens, happens. He'd returned to the States with a medal for valor under fire and the exposed areas of his skin permanently clay-colored, lizardy. Ever afterward his eyes would appear lighter than his face, spook eyes some women would call them, shivering at his touch. In the Iraqi desert he had participated in killing an indeterminate number of human beings designated as enemies, targets. These had been Iraqi soldiers of approximately his age and younger. Some of them a lot younger. He had not seen individual enemies die but he'd smelled their deaths by frying, explosion. Inhaled the unmistakable burned-meat odor, for he'd been downwind from the action, either that or not breathe. Telling of the Gulf War to those few persons to whom he spoke of such matters he would say the worst that had happened to him was fucking sand-flea bites. In fact, the worst that had happened was diarrhea. And one bright hallucinatory morning in the desert he saw his soul curl up and die like an inchworm in the hot sand.

At first he'd missed it. Then he forgot.

Back in the States he learned to be a cop. He got married to a girl he'd known in high school. He wasn't ambitious careerwise but he had certain goals. He saw that the civilian police were a branch of the U.S. armed services and the same authority/rank bullshit prevailed. That was all right with him, mostly. If authority merited his respect, authority had his respect. Captains, lieutenants, sergeants, detectives. They liked him on sight. They trusted him. He was an old-style cop of another era. In his patrolman's uniform he made a strong impression. It surprised him to learn that most cops in the NFPD had not fired their weapons at any human targets let alone killed these targets let alone felt good about it and though he would not tell anyone on the force about his Persian Gulf experience, for he was not a man to talk much about himself, somehow he exuded that air.

Yet his first partner, an older, paunch-bellied cop who had not advanced beyond patrol after eighteen years on the force, requested another partner after only three weeks.

"Guy like Dromoor, no question he's smart, he's a born cop. But he's too quiet. He don't talk, it makes you talk too much. And when he don't answer you then after a while you can't talk either, then you start thinking too much. That ain't good."

In the NFPD he had bad luck at first. But usually balanced by good.

He was hurt, sure. Pissed. That his first partner had dumped him. His second partner, a guy nearer his age, hadn't lasted long either. Not Dromoor's fault, just bad luck.

He'd been on the force just seven weeks. It was a domestic disturbance call. Late one muggy August night on the East Side where the smoke haze from the chemical factories makes your eyes sting and breathing hurt. Dromoor was driving the patrol car. As he and his partner J. J. pulled up outside a bungalow, an individual looking to be a white male, midthirties, was pulling away from the curb in a rust-stippled Ford van. It was J. J.'s call to pursue the van. What was inside the bungalow would be discovered by a backup team. The chase lasted eight minutes involving speeds of sixty, sixty-five miles an hour along narrow, potholed residential streets in that part of the city of Niagara Falls few tourists have discovered. At last the van skidded, fishtailed, collided with parked cars, and the driver was thrown against the front windshield, lay slumped over the steering wheel. There was reason to think he was unconscious. Very possibly he was dead. The windshield was cracked, there was no movement inside the cab. There came J. J. and Dromoor behind him, both with guns drawn. J. J. was anxious, excitable. Dromoor perceived that this was not a familiar experience for him. J. J. called out for the driver of the van to lift his arms from the wheel, keep his hands in sight, stay in the vehicle but keep his hands in sight. The driver of the van was unresponsive. He appeared to be bleeding from a head wound. Yet somehow it happened, Dromoor would replay the incident many times afterward seeking the key to how precisely it happened, that the driver of the van stooped to retrieve a .45-caliber revolver from beneath his seat and opened fire on J. J. through the side window as J. J. approached; and there was J. J. suddenly down in the street, a bullet in the chest. Dromoor, approximately three feet behind his partner, was struck by a second bullet in his left shoulder before he heard the *crack!* before he felt the impact of the bullet which carried no immediate pain with it, no clear sensation other than a rude, hard hit, as if he'd been clubbed with a sledgehammer. Dromoor was on one knee as the driver climbed out of the van, preparing to fire again, except Dromoor swiftly fired at him from his kneeling position, upward at an angle, three bullets each of which struck the shooter in the head.

This was John Dromoor's first kill in the NFPD. It would not be his last.

The Friend

People you meet, most of them make little impression. Others, they make a strong impression. Even if you don't meet them again, if your paths don't cross. Still.

She recognized him from local TV, newspapers. His face, that is. His name she would not have recognized, though it was a strange name and one she murmured aloud, smiling: "Dro-moor."

At the Horseshoe Bar & Grill they were introduced. This was not long after Dromoor's citation for valor, a public ceremony covered by local TV, newspapers. Dromoor was credited with saving the life of his partner in a shooting and such events, though not rare in the sprawling city of Buffalo close by, were rare enough in the depopulated city of Niagara Falls to draw media interest. Yet Dromoor refused to talk much about what he'd done. You did not perceive him as a modest man, rather a man largely indifferent to others' opinions of him as he was indifferent to others' opinions of all things. When Teena Maguire congratulated him on the citation, Dromoor said, without irony, "That was back in August." It was mid-September now.

The Horseshoe had once been a Falls supper club, glitzy, glamorous. In the economic recessions of the waning twentieth century it had devolved into a neighborhood tavern, favored by cops and courthouse staff. Martine Maguire—Teena to her friends—was known there. She was a widow with a young daughter. Many of the regular customers at the Horseshoe had known her husband, Ross Maguire. He had worked at Goodyear Tire, he'd died of a quickly spreading melanoma cancer several years before. A few of the men at the Horseshoe had dated Teena. Possibly there'd been some emotional entanglements. But no lingering resentments. Teena was well liked, admired. She was flirtatious without being aggressive. She got along with women as easily as she got along with men, single women like herself, dropping by the Horseshoe on a Friday evening after work.

By chance she'd met Dromoor that evening. He was new to the NFPD and to Niagara Falls. She would recall afterward that he'd said very little to her, but he had listened. She'd had the impression he was moved by hearing she was a widow, and so young. And she had a daughter to raise alone. When Dromoor offered to buy her a drink and Teena declined, he didn't insist. Though they remained together at the bar. There was no one else there who so interested them as they interested each other. Dromoor drank ale. Dark ale from the tap. His eyes were lighter than his face, which appeared masklike, like baked clay. Near the end of the evening, as Teena was about to leave, she told Dromoor he should call her sometime, if he had the time. Dromoor frowned and told her in a lowered voice so that no one else at the bar could hear that he'd like that, except he was married and his wife was having their first baby in about twenty days.

Teena laughed, and said she appreciated that. Being told.

"John Dromoor. You're my friend."

She leaned upward to kiss his cheek. Brush her lips across his baked-clay cheek. Just a touch, a gesture. She'd really liked this guy, and she guessed he liked her, to a degree. But this was it. No more than this. The next time Teena Maguire and John Dromoor were in such close proximity to each other it would be nearly two years later in the boathouse at Rocky Point Park and Teena Maguire would be unconscious.

Luck

Hʟᴏᴡ ᴀ ʟɪꜰᴇ ɪꜱ decided. How a life is ended.

Good luck, bad luck. Purely luck.

When your mother leaned over you to blow into your ear. "Bethie-baby! Let's go."

It was a few minutes before midnight, Fourth of July 1996.

You'd fallen asleep on the creaky outdoor sofa on Casey's front porch. After the fireworks ended on the river. Waiting for your mother to leave but the party wasn't showing signs of winding down.

Your face smarted from sunburn. Eyes burned in their sockets. It had been a long giddy day: like a roller-coaster ride. Momma was laughing at you saying she'd better get you home to bed, it was almost midnight.

You objected you were okay. You weren't a little kid. You didn't want to go home yet.

Casey said, sliding his arm around your mother's shoulders in a fierce-playful hug, "Bethie can sleep upstairs if she wants to. There's room. Stay a while longer, Teena? C'mon."

Momma was tempted. She was having a good time, she loved casual neighborhood parties. And she loved Casey, sort of.

But Momma decided *no*.

Like Mother, Like Daughter

You were Bethel Maguire everybody called Bethie. Your childhood ended when you were twelve years old.

Always you would think *If*. If Momma had not said *no*.

You'd have stayed at Casey's that night. Both of you. And what would happen in Rocky Point Park would not happen and no one would have knowledge of the possibility of its having happened and so your childhood would not have ended that night.

Good luck, bad luck. Hit by lightning, spared by lightning.

Mostly you liked the neighborhood parties, summer picnics that began in backyards and spilled out into the street. Amplified music. Rock, country-and-western, bluegrass. Ray Casey favored bluegrass and if you were a friend of Casey's you got to like it, too. As Momma said either that or plug up your ears.

At Casey's that night lots of people were dancing. Just disco-dancing, wild and fun. Teena Maguire was one of the best dancers, no guy could keep up with her. Only other women.

That Teena! Look at her!

Teena's hot tonight!

Often you were told that you'd inherited Teena Maguire's

17

tawny-blond hair and fair skin. Except you knew you weren't pretty like Teena and never would be.

Watching Momma dance and flirt and laugh so hard her eyes were shut to slits, seeing how other people looked at her, you worried sometimes. That Teena Maguire made a certain impression that wasn't exactly her.

Drinking too much at these parties. Acting kind of breathless, excited. Like a high school girl not a woman in her midthirties. (So old! You were too fastidious to wish to know your mother's exact age.) Her tank top slipping off her shoulder, you could see Teena wasn't wearing a bra beneath.

Her hair, scissor-cut in layers, which she'd had "lightened," falling into her eyes.

Her skin that, if you touched, you could feel: heat lifting from it.

Her laughter, in surprised-sounding peals like glass breaking.

You knew: your mother deserved some good times. She was really nice compared to most of your friends' mothers. She loved you, and it wasn't any exaggeration she'd do anything for you. She missed your father but did not wish to dwell on the past. She did not complain, anyway not much. Her favored remark was *Things could be a helluva lot worse* delivered with a TV-comic shrug. She was under a lot of tension at her job, receptionist for two bossy dentists who were always critical of her. And there was her own mother depending on her to visit sometimes twice a day and wanting her and you to move in with her in the brick house on Baltic Avenue.

Momma protested she could not! Just could not.

It would be the easy thing to do. Move back in with

Grandma. Of course she would save money but then she would never remarry. Her life would be over, her life as a woman. She could not bear that.

Your mother was a woman who liked men. Sometimes, too much.

Had it coming. Asked for it. Everybody knows what she was.

Over the years there'd been a number of men in your mother's life and yet none had ever stayed overnight in your house on Ninth Street. Your mother wouldn't allow this, she didn't want to upset you.

Not that she'd told you this. But you figured.

Now it was Ray Casey, your mother had been seeing for about a year.

Were Momma and Casey going to get married? You could not ask.

You told Momma you liked Casey a lot, which was true. You told her it was okay with you if they got married but really it was not.

If they got married, if Momma brought you to live in Casey's house, you believed that Momma would love you less. Momma would have less time for you. Momma would love *him*.

You were jealous of Casey, sometimes you wished Casey would get back together with his wife. Or move away. Or die.

Four years seven months since Ross Maguire your father had died yet you thought of him a lot. More like the idea of *Dad, Daddy* sometimes than any actual memory. When you were fully awake, his face was kind of blurred. But drifting off to sleep you would see him, suddenly! You would hear his voice, the deep, comforting sound of his voice, you would see his face, his smile, you felt his presence in the house. Before he'd gotten sick and went to the hospital and did not return there'd been two times: the feel of the house when Daddy was there, and when Daddy was not there.

It would be wrong. It would be not-right. For another man to pretend to be your daddy.

Some mean-mouthed people in the neighborhood were saying that Ray Casey had left his wife for Teena Maguire but that was *not true*. Casey's wife had left Niagara Falls, with their children. Moved back to live with her family in Corning, New York. It was a hard commute for Casey to see his kids. He was hurt, he was disgusted. He was baffled what he'd done wrong. His marriage was finished, he said. His marriage was dead. Casey had a way of saying *dead!* with a certain vehemence. He would say he was crazy in love with Teena Maguire. *Crazy in love* uttered with a certain vehemence, too.

It would be said that Teena Maguire had had a quarrel with her boyfriend Casey that night. That's why she left the party, took her daughter, and went to walk home. That's why she was in Rocky Point Park at midnight. *They were drunk, fighting. She ran off. He let her go.*

Just after dark the fireworks display began on the Niagara River a mile and a half away. A few kids went upstairs in Casey's house, climbed out the front windows to squat on the porch to see the dazzling lights, you were one of them, hoping your mother wouldn't notice.

She did, though. Or somebody tipped her off.

"Bethie, get down! Damn you, get down before you break your neck."

You protested the roof was practically flat, you weren't going to fall off, but Momma insisted, threatening to come upstairs and get you. It was embarrassing how much fuss your mother was making over you on a porch roof not fifteen feet from the ground but this was typical of her obsessing about your safety. Casey tried to make a joke of it saying you could jump down and he'd catch you, like a fireman.

In fact, Casey was a volunteer fireman.

Naturally, your mother got her way. You were mortified having to crawl back up the roof and through the window, while the other kids watched. Rolling your eyes, muttering, "Damn my mother, she's always bossing me around. Treats me like some stupid kid five years old." You sounded harsher than you meant. Really it was meant to be funny.

Later, after the fireworks ended, you must have fallen asleep on the rattan sofa. Amid the loud music and raised voices and laughter you slept for about an hour until your mother stooped to blow into your ear, waking you.

"Bethie. Time to go home, sweetie."

"I wasn't asleep. . . ."

You were confused at first, your face throbbed with sunburn.

More than twelve hours before you'd been playing soft-ball in the park. Swimming in the pool that was jammed with screaming kids, and exposed to the hot sun. Your stomach was queasy, all the delicious corn on the cob you'd eaten. Casey's grilled hamburgers, Momma's potato salad with slices of hard–boiled egg. Carrot cake, ice cream. God knows how many soft drinks out of the ice chest in the backyard.

The daughter was drinking beer, too. Like mother, like daughter in that family.

There was a final shake of the dice. Another time it might have been averted. When Casey said, "Teena, let me drive you two home. Wait a minute, I'll get the car," and your mother thanked him and kissed him on the cheek, telling him not to bother—"We want to walk, don't we, Bethie? It's a perfect night."

The Boathouse

By 1:25 A.M. of July 5, 1996, it would be cordoned off by Niagara Falls police as a crime scene.

It was a low shingleboard service building beside the Rocky Point lagoon. It was used for the storage of park equipment: rowboats and canoes not in use, picnic tables, benches, folding chairs, trash barrels. In the interior there was a smell of stagnant water, rodents, rotting wood. There was a lingering odor of stale urine, for homeless men sometimes slept here.

On the filthy floor near the front entrance, the gang-rape victim would almost die. It would be speculated that she'd been left to die. If her rapists had been thinking, not so drunk, or so drugged, not so excited, they'd have made sure she was dead. And her twelve-year-old daughter who'd crawled behind the stacked boats to hide.

A witness. Two witnesses! To identify the rapists, testify against them.

But the rapists hadn't been thinking. They had not had time to think and they were not in a state to think. Had not thought out what they would do to their thirty-five-year-old victim beyond the frenzied act of doing.

The Lagoon

B𝐲 day you sometimes bicycled along this path. Alone, or with friends. Weeping willow branches brushed against your face, whiplike. The brick path was uneven, bumpy. In the corner of your eye you saw the figures of homeless men slumped against the service buildings, or lying seemingly comatose on the grass. By day, you felt no danger.

By night, the path was lighted. But half the lights had been broken or were burned out.

Still you could see the surface of the lagoon. Moonlight reflected in broken patches. The water was covered in a faint scum that rippled and shivered like the skin of a nervous beast. The sky was gauzy drifting clouds high overhead. Near the Falls there was always mist, clouds of vapor. You could see the moon's battered face, what looked like a winking eye.

It would have been a ten-minute walk through Rocky Point Park, from Casey's house to your house. Except Momma wanted to take the lagoon path. Where it was *so pretty.*

Saying in her happy-wistful voice you dreaded, "Your father used to take the three of us out in a rowboat on the lagoon, Bethie, do you remember? Sometimes just him and you in a canoe. You took your dolls along."

"I always hated dolls, Momma."

On the lagoon were scattered feathers. No swans, no mallards or geese, must've been sleeping in the rushes at shore. Or maybe kids tossing firecrackers had caused them to fly away.

On the other side of the park, the high school baseball game had long ended. The bright lights on thirty-foot poles at the field had long been extinguished. The bleachers were empty and most of the park was deserted. There was little traffic on the roadways. Now and then you would hear the rapid-fire *crack-crack-crack!* of firecrackers and young-male laughter.

Beer cans and litter floating in the lagoon. Still it was beautiful by moonlight, Teena Maguire insisted.

The ornamental stucco facade of the waterworks was lighted. This was an old "historic" building designed by a renowned architect and in its derelict state it retained still some measure of dignity. Dark brick, cream-colored stucco, mortar now badly crumbling. Once-elegant iron scrollwork over the windows and doors. Heroic stone figures in recessed alcoves and at the edge of the roof: nude male warriors with swords and shields, females with blank faces and hair to their waists. One of them was a mermaid with a ridiculous curving fish tail instead of legs.

You asked your mother what's the point of a mermaid— "It's so *silly*."

You didn't want to say the mermaid scared you, somehow. Since you'd been a little girl, seeing it above the lagoon. A freaky deformed female with no legs.

Momma said, "What's the point of anything made up? Just something exotic for men to look at, I guess. Men make these things up."

"But, Momma, there has got to be some *point.*"

Suddenly you were angry with your mother. Not knowing why.

There was a small spit of land, out into the lagoon, you could walk out to see a low-built dam over which water flowed in a constant frothy stream. You hoped your mother wouldn't want to walk there, where the path was poorly lighted.

You hoped your mother wouldn't bring up the subject of your father again tonight. It wasn't the right time, July Fourth. It was meant to be a silly-happy time. An empty-headed time. At Casey's, the way Momma stared up at you on the porch roof like you were in actual danger of your life, you were so embarrassed! Teena Maguire was one to exaggerate certain things while completely ignoring others.

She was staring at the boathouse now. It was closed for the night, a metal shutter had been clamped down on the side facing the lagoon. The boathouse was covered in graffiti like deranged shouts. KIKI LOVES R. D. TO DEATH SUCK ASON FUCK YOU!!! FUK ST THOMASS.

(You'd have to be a local to know that this referred to St. Thomas Aquinas High School, on the north side of the city.)

Momma said, in a voice like she was personally hurt, annoyed, "Somebody should clean this park up, it used to be so beautiful and now it's just *sad.*"

You said, brattish twelve-year-old needing to get the last

word, "Momma, the city of Niagara Falls is *sad*. Where've you been?"

Across a roadway, through a stand of pine trees, was Ninth Street.

A five-minute walk home.

Faces rushing at you. Grinning teeth, glittery eyes.

Like a pack of dogs. So fast!

Three of them ahead of you, driving you back.

Teasing, laughing. Yipping.

One of them is bare chested. Skinny chest, hairless. A smell of something sweetly acrid, burning.

Straggly-haired, loud-laughing. Running beside you. More of them, younger kids. Clapping their hands hooting and jeering driving you and your mother back, toward the interior of the park. The boathouse.

It's happening too fast. Your eyes are open but blind.

Telling yourself this isn't happening, this will not happen.

In another minute this will stop. This will go away.

Momma is trying to talk to them. Smile at them. Joke. They seem to know her. Teeeeena! Touching her hair, grabbing at her hair. One of them, sand-colored hair in his eyes, unbuttoned red shirt falling open on a flabby fatty chest covered in wiry hairs, tries to kiss her, lunging like a barracuda with bared teeth.

Trying to joke with him. Trying to fight him off.

Five of them, or six? Another two waiting, by the boathouse, where they've forced a door open.

Neighborhood guys, familiar faces. The one in the red shirt is a face you know.

Momma pleading please guys leave us alone, okay? Please don't hurt us, don't hurt my daughter please she's just a little girl, okay, guys?

Hands clutching at you. Your hair, the nape of your neck. You try to duck away and a dark-haired boy blocks you gleefully, arms out-stretched like it's a basketball game, you've got the ball and he's the guard towering over you.

The guys are laughing at Momma crying, begging for them to leave her daughter alone, screaming Bethie run! Honey, get away!

They let you break free, run a few yards, then catch you. So hard your arm is wrenched put of its socket. It's a game.

They let your mother break free, run barefoot and stumbling in the grass, then catch her. Three of them, like drunken dancers.

Hey there foxy lady, whereya goin'?

Mmmmm good-lookin' show us your titties foxy lady hey-heyHEY.

Dragging you into the boathouse. Your mother, and you. You're fighting them, kicking wildly and trying to scream but there's a hot sweaty salt-tasting hand clamped over your mouth.

The last you hear of your mother sobbing is Don't! Don't hurt her! Let her go!

In Hiding

WEDGED IN A CORNER of the boathouse. Behind, partially beneath stacked upside-down canoes.

You'd crawled desperate to escape. On your stomach, on raw-scraped elbows. Dragging yourself like a wounded snake. As one of them kicked you. Cursed you kicking your back, your thighs, your legs as if he wanted to break all your bones in his fury.

You'd twisted out of his grip. So small-boned, so skinny. No breasts, no hips. Not enough female flesh to grab on to.

Where's the little cunt, where the fuck is she hiding? . . .

Wedged in the farthest corner of the boathouse. In the darkness smelling of stagnant water, soft-rotted wood. A sharp stink of urine. You were in terror of choking, suffocating. You'd squeezed into a space so small, your body was bent double. Your knees were drawn up against your chest, your shoulders hunched. Above you and to the side, stacked in tiers, were upside-down canoes. If they'd fallen, you would have been crushed.

In terror of what they were doing to your mother. What you would have to endure, hearing.

You did not think *rape*. The word *rape* was not yet a word in your vocabulary.

You would think *beat, hurt. Try to kill.*

You heard your mother's cries, stifled screams. You heard her pleading with them. You heard them laugh at her.

Teeeeena! Show your titties now Teeeena.

Spread your legs Teeeena. Your cunt.

You heard them kicking your mother. Soft-thudding blows against unresisting flesh. They would grab your mother's slender ankles, spread her legs violently as if they wished to tear her legs from her body. They laughed at her cries of pain, her terror. They laughed at her feeble attempts to protect herself. They were reckless, euphoric. You would learn that they were high on a drug called crystal meth. In their excitement they forgot you. You were of no significance to them, who had an adult woman. They had torn your mother's clothes from her body as if the female's clothes infuriated them. They spat in your mother's face as if her beauty infuriated them. They yanked at your mother's hair wishing to pull it out by the roots. One of them would gouge repeatedly at her right eye with his thumb, wishing to blind her. You could not know how there was a radiant madness in their faces, a glisten to their wolf-eyes, a sheen to their damp teeth. You could not know how their eyes showed rims of white above the irises. How their bodies were coated in oily sweat. How they straddled your mother's limp body and jammed their penises into her bleeding mouth and into her bleeding vagina and into her bleeding rectum. You would hear the noises of this rape not fully aware that what you heard was *rape*. You were fainting with pain from your dislocated arm, you were trying to breathe through the cracks in the splintery filthy floorboards. A few inches beneath these floorboards the scummy water of the lagoon lapped, rippled. You pressed the scraped and bleeding palms of your hands against your ears for twenty minutes and more begging *God don't let them kill Momma please God help us please.*

"Gang Rape"

THE CALL CAME IN at 12:58 A.M. It was the third call of the night dispatching Zwaaf and Dromoor to the vicinity of Rocky Point Park.

This crazed Fourth of July. Since dusk, NFPD sirens had mingled with the sirens of medical vehicles summoned to emergencies. There were fire sirens, burglar and car alarms. There were exploding fireworks at the Niagara River, in the publicly sanctioned annual display, and there were illegal detonating firecrackers through the city. There were reports of gunshots. Tourists to the Falls reported muggings, petty thefts from their broken-into vehicles parked in the large municipal lots near the river. Tourists in the hotels reported room break-ins, thefts. A record number of individuals, mostly male, mostly young, injured themselves and others setting off illegal fireworks and firecrackers. There were complaints of youths tossing lighted firecrackers through the windows of houses and passing vehicles. There were complaints of terrorized dogs and cats. There were complaints from boaters lodged against other, aggressive and drunken boaters. There were complaints of bands of drunken and/or drug-addled youths, Caucasian, African-American, Hispanic, congregating in the city's parks. There were drug arrests, arrests for public drunkenness and drunken driving, public prostitution, solicitation, lewd and lascivious behavior. There were scattered fires, some of them suspicious. There were barbecue accidents and swimming pool accidents. There were arrests beneath the bleachers at the Rocky Point baseball field, in the men's lavatories and in the parking lots. A considerable quantity of controlled substances was confiscated by police officers, predominantly marijuana, cocaine, and a powerful synthetic drug newly popular in the Niagara region, meth amphetamine.

Meth was the worst. Fried and sizzled the brain.

Zwaaf said, disgusted, "Any asshole who wants drugs, they should lock 'em up and give it to them. Let 'em kill themselves and good riddance."

Zwaaf and his younger partner Dromoor had made several of these arrests. Petty drug dealers, at the park. Other arrests that night had been for drunk driving, youths involved in muggings, assaults. A few weapons had been confiscated. Illegal fireworks. Fourth of July was a perverse holiday, Zwaaf believed. He'd come to hate it. He was a veteran of the NFPD patrol scene. His mood oscillated between scorn and dismay. He looked forward to retirement yet there were scores to settle. He behaved toward Dromoor in the way of an elder brother of an inscrutable youth whose differences from himself he wished to ignore. He complained to Dromoor that Dromoor was too fucking quiet even as he, Zwaaf, talked nonstop. Of the Fourth of July he complained it was a holiday with no point except breaking the law with fires, explosions, noises indistinguishable from gunshots. Dangerous and out-of-control like New Year's Eve at midnight except worse than fucking New Year's Eve because July was summer and everybody was out on the street.

Dromoor only half-listened to Artie Zwaaf. Dromoor was not thinking that this Fourth of July was out-of-control, yet. There was something to come, maybe. To Dromoor always there was something-to-come. He was restless, edgy. He drove the patrol car which gave him something to do every minute, but still. He did not cherish quiet times. He had domestic problems of which he would not speak to Artie Zwaaf who was not to be trusted with confidences even if Dromoor was a man to confide in another which certainly he was not. Dromoor did not think his problems were profound or even unusual. He supposed that they were not even insoluble. They were vexing the way a too-tight collar is vexing around a dog's neck, that the dog can feel but can't see. Dromoor was becoming impatient patrolling the pot-holed Niagara Falls streets. He had hopes for moving up in the NFPD. He was the father of an eighteen-month infant and would be the father of a second infant in less than seven months. As a cop he had not been in personal danger since the shooting involving J. J. on that August night nearly two years before, he had scarcely had cause to draw his gun. He had not had cause to fire. But this Fourth of July night, the arrests he and Zwaaf had made had been without incident. Even the drug-addled had not resisted. No one had resisted arrest, even initially. No one had struggled when he was cuffed. No one had suddenly shoved at the officers, tried to run away. No one had wished to turn his back on the officers and run away. At the park, approaching a noisy crowd of black and Hispanic youths, Dromoor had wielded his nightstick. But he had not needed to use it.

This call from Rocky Point Park. A 911 from a motorist who'd been stopped on a roadway by a child, a young girl of approximately eleven/twelve, disheveled, torn clothing, bleeding at the nose and mouth, saying her mother had been beaten, hurt bad, in the boathouse at the lagoon. And when they'd arrived at the site, there was the girl dazed sitting on the grass, and Dromoor saw the look of her, the torn clothing, bloodied face, the way one of her arms hung wrongly, and knew it must be rape.

Medics were arriving. Dromoor and Zwaaf would be first to enter the boathouse. In the harsh unsparing light of their flashlights the naked woman lay open-mouthed, open-legged in the supplicant posture of death. She was scarcely breathing, almost imperceptibly her rib cage lifted and fell. She was bleeding from head wounds, a broken nose, torn lips. A pool of dark blood lay beneath her, spreading from between her legs. Her fingernails, which had been polished a glamorous gleaming crimson, matching her painted toenails, were jagged and broken. Her eyelids were only partially closed. Tears or mucus encrusted her lashes. Her hair, a tawny blond, was splotched with blood. Her breasts, which were full, heavy, lay partially flattened against her chest, and were also smeared with blood in the way of savage and exotic tattoos.

Zwaaf muttered, "Jesus! They really got her."

Dromoor was squatting beside the unconscious woman. His flashlight shook in his awkwardly uplifted hand. Here, he amended, was rape. This was the rape. The other, the girl, the daughter, had been beaten but not raped.

He had never been called to the scene of a gang rape before. He had never seen the victim of a gang rape except in photographs. He would not forget the sight.

He knew the woman's name: Martine Maguire.

Teena, she was called. Lived in the neighborhood. A widow.

Since their meeting at the Horseshoe, Dromoor had seen Teena Maguire a few times, at a distance. He had kept that distance between them believing it was to no purpose, otherwise. She had not seen him.

Medics entered the boathouse. The scene was swathed in unnatural light more radiant than the sun.

Witness

Y ou were twelve at the time. Your thirteenth birthday would arrive abruptly, too soon in August, and depart mostly unheralded. For childhood belonged to *before*, now you had come to live in *after*.

You would tell what you could remember.

Many times you would tell. And retell.

That night, the very night of the rape, in the emergency room at St. Mary's where you and your unconscious mother were taken by ambulance, you were questioned. Before your grandmother and other relatives arrived at the hospital, you were questioned. You were eager to tell. All that you knew. You were desperate to cooperate. In the way of childish logic you believed that all that you could do would help your mother to live.

Though one day Teena Maguire would curse the fact that she'd been kept alive, five days on a respirator and attached to IV tubes in intensive care at St. Mary's, had not been put out of her misery with a bullet to the brain there on the boat-house floor, fucking bad luck she'd ever been born.

The Enemy

Y<small>OU WERE INSTRUCTED</small> *Take your time, Bethie.*

At the Eighth Precinct where police officers showed you photographs.

Grandma brought you. From St. Mary's to the police station she brought you. Your mother was still unconscious, on a life-support system. You were the sole witness.

Trying to explain it happened so fast.

So fast! And it was so dark! The men's faces . . .

Your mouth was sore, swollen. Every word you uttered hurt.

There was a woman, not one of the detectives but a Family Services counselor. She smiled at you the way a kindergarten teacher might smile at her pupils. Telling you in a slow, careful voice that just because things had happened fast to you did not mean that you had to remember anything "fast."

Take your time, Bethie. This is very very important.

So many pictures of young men and boys! Some of them were very young-looking, like kids from Baltic High. Some of the faces were familiar, or almost.

Mostly these were white men. The rapists had all been white. Except dark-skinned, unshaven, with dark hair, heavy eyebrows. It scared you now, you could not have described their *race*. You would have to say white. White-but-dark. Darkish-skinned but white. You would have to say . . .

Remembering how he'd kicked you. Kick-kick-kicked your back, your thighs and legs, laughing, trying to grab your ankles, clumsy and stumbling and giving up, the little cunt wasn't worth the effort.

If you found his face here! He would come back to kill you.

He was the enemy. They were all the enemy. They knew your name, they knew your mother's name. And where you lived, they knew. You began to shiver, you could not stop shivering. Your eyes were wet with tears. The detectives stared at you in silence. The Family Services woman took your hands, gently.

Calling you Bethie. Saying it was all right you would be safe.

The police would protect you, she said. You and your mother, the police will protect you. Please believe us.

You did not believe. You did not know what to believe.

You continued to look at the pictures. Saw a familiar face, and pointed: him?

No. Changed your mind. No, maybe not. They looked so much like one another, guys you saw every day on the street.

At the 7-Eleven where Momma was always shopping. At the Huron Shopping Center. Driving by on Ninth Street these muggy hot summer evenings, and through the park, a hallf-dozen yelling, hooting guy hanging out of a noisy old car with oversized tires.

This one! Suddenly, you were sure.

The guy with the sand-colored hair falling in his face. Sexy like a rock star except his face was broken out in pimples.

Jeering and nasty he'd been, rushing at you. Grabbing at your mother and trying to kiss her. Grabbing at her breasts. Teeeena!

You realized now, he'd led the others. He was their leader. You knew.

This one. Yes.

Almost, you knew this guy's name. Pick?

On Eleventh Street near the lumberyard there was a family named Pick living in a large yellow-tile house. The front yard was grassless, but the driveway was crammed with vehicles—cars, motorcycles, a motorboat on a trailer. Leila Pick was three years older than you at Baltic Junior High, a fattish, aggressive girl. There were older brothers in the family, one of them named Marvin.

Excited, you knew this was him: Marvin Pick.

Later you would identify his brother, though you didn't know his name: Lloyd. The Pick features were unmistakable. A wide-boned face, thick nose with dark nostrils. A low forehead, sand-colored hair.

Marvin Pick was twenty-six; his brother Lloyd was twenty-four.

Here! This one, too.

Jimmy DeLucca, this young man would be. It scared you to see his picture close up. Sneering at Momma in his angry, nasty voice, *Cunt dirty cunt show us your titties cunt!*

You would not find the one who'd kicked you. He'd had

a mustache, stubbled jaw. The imprint of his angry fingers in bruised welts on your ankles. *Whereya goin' you little cunt?!*

Except: the detectives said to try again. And you did. And there he was.

"Suspects," they were called. As if they hadn't done what they'd done to you and your mother but were only "suspected" of doing it!

You identified just five of them. By their mug shots, and in lineups at the precinct. Staring at groups of six to eight young men through a one-way window. Assured that they couldn't see you though you saw them. In the bright unsparing lights of the viewing room, the rapists were not so confident. Their mouths were not so jeering. Their eyes were not so glassy-hard.

Immediately you saw them, you knew them. You understood then that you would never forget those faces.

There had been others. Maybe seven, eight. Maybe more. It had been so confusing. And others had come, drawn by the commotion. Out of the park. From the roadway. Maybe.

You could positively identify just five. These had been the most aggressive, the first to rush at you.

Marvin Pick. Lloyd Pick. Jimmy DeLucca. Fritz Haaber. Joe Rickert.

Each of these young men had police records in Niagara County for petty crimes. All had juvenile records sealed by Family Court. Both Picks and DeLucca had served time in a juvenile facility. Haaber had been on probation in 1994 for having assaulted his girlfriend. Rickert was on parole from Olean Men's Correctional Facility, where he'd served time for robbery and drug possession.

All of the suspects lived in the Twelfth Street/Huron Avenue neighborhood of the city, east of Rocky Point Park. About a mile from where you and your mother lived on Ninth Street.

So close! You would not wish to think how close.

After you'd identified the suspects, you were told that they had already been taken into custody by police in the early hours of July 5. Along with numerous other young men they had been brought to the precinct for questioning in the gang rape/assault. It was clear to police that many of the detained men knew about the rape whether they had participated in it or not. "Word gets around. These guys know one another." Clothing and shoes belonging to some of the men had been confiscated for examination. Bloodstains on these items would be matched against your mother's blood and your own, as semen found in and upon your mother's body would be matched against the suspects' DNA.

Skin tissue beneath your mother's broken nails would be matched against their DNA.

It was possible that more suspects would be brought in, the detectives said. "These punks, they'll inform on one another if they think they can save their sorry asses."

The police investigation had begun without your knowledge, like a great eye opening.

Defense

IT IS A FACT, the suspects' lawyers would insist. Bethel Maguire is twelve years old. Bethel Maguire was confused, panicked at the time of the assault. Bethel Maguire had not witnessed any actual act of rape perpetrated upon her mother, for she had been by her own admission in hiding during the rape, in a corner of the boathouse in darkness.

She had not seen any rape. She had seen only the blurred, uncertain faces of a number of young men, in the park outside the boathouse.

The path beside the lagoon was poorly lighted. The interior of the boathouse was not lighted at all.

How can the child be sure? How can we believe her? How can a child of twelve swear? How can a child of twelve testify?

"That Girl, Teena Maguire's Daughter"

A s soon as your mother and you were dragged into the boathouse at Rocky Point Park you began to exist in *after*. Never again could you exist in *before*. That time of your childhood before you and your mother became victims was gone forever, remote as a scene glimpsed at a distance, fading like vapor as you stare in longing.

"Momma! Momma don't die! Momma I love you don't *die*."

You had thought she was dead, on the boathouse floor. Crawling to her. To where they'd left her. Racked in pain, frantic. You had hidden in the darkest corner of the boathouse and you had pressed your hands over your ears and you had heard the ugly sounds of your mother being assaulted and you had reason to believe that you had heard the sounds of her death and so through your life it would seem to you that your mother had died, and you had been a witness to her death who had died, too.

After would be years. You are still living those years. *After* would be the remainder of your mother's life.

* * *

WHAT YOU DIDN'T REALIZE. What no one could have told you. How the rape was not an incident that had happened one night in the park in the random way of a stroke of lightning but the very definition of Teena Maguire's life, and by extension your life, afterward. What had been Teena, what had been Bethie, was suddenly eclipsed. Your mother would be *That woman who was gang-raped in the boathouse at Rocky Point Park* and you would be *That girl, Teena Maguire's daughter.*

Off-Duty

Dromoor dropped by St. Mary's. Inquired at the front desk how a patient named Maguire was doing, in intensive care.

The heavily made-up receptionist frowned into a computer. Type-type-typing rapidly. Frowned importantly saying such information was confidential unless he was a family member, and was he?

Dromoor considered showing the woman his badge. Saying he'd been the officer to first see Martine Maguire. He'd been the one to see what had been done to her. And so he had a right to know if she would live.

The receptionist was staring at Dromoor, waiting. He'd been so still, his thoughts had plunged inward.

"Sir? Are you a family member? Or . . ."

Dromoor shook his head no. Turned and walked away. Fuck it he couldn't get involved, he had promised himself. Married and a father and his wife already anxious about him and he wasn't the type, not the type to get involved.

The Vigil

At St. Mary's. Visiting hours from 8:30 A.M. until 11:00 P.M. now that your mother is out of intensive care and in a private room on the fourth floor.

Grandma is paying extra for the private room, which Momma's insurance won't pay for. Grandma and you, you practically live at St. Mary's now. *God only let my daughter live. God help us in our hour of need. God have mercy on us. Let my daughter live. I will never ask anything of You again.*

At first it was not known whether Teena Maguire would ever recover what is circumspectly called "consciousness." After two days at St. Mary's you were released but your mother remained on a life support system in the intensive care unit, her condition was "critical." In a coma, for her skull had been "concussed." There had been "pinpoint hemorrhaging" in her brain. She was not able to breathe on her own. She was fed intravenously. A catheter drained toxins from her body in a continual thin stream. Speaking to your grandmother, the neurologist was awkward, evasive. It was like a bad joke hearing this professional in his hospital whites utter such words as *We can only hope for the best.*

You saw hope rising into the sky. A flimsy kite torn by the winds off Lake Ontario. You laughed, you were so scared.

Then, on the morning of the sixth day of the vigil, your mother began to open her eyes. She began to wake, intermittently. All that day and into the next. You could feel Momma forcing herself up out of sleep like a swimmer breaking the surface of a heavy viscous water like molten lead. You could feel her effort, the tremulous strength of her will. Her bruised eyelids fluttered. Her wounded mouth quivered. "Momma!" you whispered. You were holding one of her icy hands, Grandma was holding the other. "Teena! We're here, honey. Bethie and me. Both of us. We won't leave you. We love you."

Eventually your mother woke from her sleep. At first she was childlike, trusting. What had happened to her was vague as an explosion or a car crash or a building collapsing on her head. Her shaved head swathed in white gauze and her chalky-pale skin had a look of something newborn you wished only to protect.

Childhood was over and yet: as long as your mother could not remember what had happened to her you could behave in the old way of *before.*

Casey came, after several days. Gaunt and poorly shaved and strangely shy, swallowing hard. On the street it was known what had happened to Teena Maguire, in the newspapers it had been more delicately expressed. To Casey's face no one would wish to say *That Maguire woman, she had it coming.*

Casey's visits with Teena Maguire were brief and very awkward. In his shaky hands he brought flowers hastily purchased in the hospital gift shop. The first time, a dozen waxy-red roses. The second time, a tinfoil-wrapped pot of white mums. His moist eyes stared and stared at the swollen-faced bruised-eyed woman in the hospital bed. He loved Teena Maguire but you could see that he was terrified of what was hidden beneath the white gauze that tightly covered her head. He was terrified of what injuries, the worst of them internal, had been done to her in that part of her body hidden by bedclothes. The last he'd seen of Teena Maguire they'd all been drinking and happy celebrating the Fourth of July. The last he'd seen of Teena Maguire she'd been another woman. Leaning to kiss his cheek saying *Love ya, Casey! Call me in the morning.*

There had been no next morning. For Casey and Teena there would never be another next morning.

The room is filling up with flowers and cards. Even when Casey ceases to visit, he will send a floral bouquet from the gift shop downstairs. A card signed *Love, Casey.*

A few of the nurses at St. Mary's know your mother from high school when she was Teena Kevecki. They drop by the room to see her, trained not to show surprise, shock, embarrassment, or indignation at the sight of any patient. Trained to call out, "Teena, hello! How are they treating you here?"

When relatives enter the room, it isn't the same. Their eyes fix on your mother's battered face and swathed head. They search for words that elude them. The women take Grandma aside to ask cautiously if Teena will have permanent facial scars. They ask about the mysterious "internal" injuries.

You don't hear Grandma's replies. You try not to hear.

Can't sleep except when Momma sleeps. Can't eat except when Momma eats. Can't smile except if Momma smiles with her swollen, lacerated mouth.

You are reverting to childish behavior, you want only to crawl into bed beside your mother and be held by her. Though Momma is not strong enough to hold you or comfort you or even kiss you unless you poke your fevered face close to hers, against her wounded mouth.

Your arm! Yanked out of its socket with a *crack!* you imagined you had heard. Now it has been forced back into its socket yet still you are in pain much of the time, your arm feels useless to you like a dead girl's arm. Your eyes are reddened from crying. Your back, sides, thighs are covered in bruises from where the one named Haaber kicked you. *Where's the little cunt where the fuck is she hiding?* But in Momma's hospital room you are safe, and you can sleep. Patches of sleep drift by like clouds. You smile seeing Momma's dreams fleeting and shining like vapor. *Momma wait! Take me with you.* Lower your head to rest it on your crossed arms, on the bed. Next thing you know Grandma has come into the room waking you. A nurse is bringing Momma's dinner on a tray, her soft-diet food.

Momma lets you help her with her meals. Though by now she can feed herself. Apple juice, bouillon, puréed carrots like baby food. And strawberry Jell-O. So delicious, you and Momma plan you will make Jell-O all the time when she comes home.

Outside your mother's room you overhear one nurse asking another *That poor girl, the daughter. They didn't rape her, too, did they?*

"Bethie? Something happened to us, I guess? But you're all right, honey? Are you?"

Momma is so anxious, you tell her *yesyes!*

She sleeps so much. In the midst of watching TV her head droops, she's asleep. You want to snuggle beside her. You want the vigil never to end.

One day in reproach pinching your arm as if she's only just thought of this: "Bethie, you didn't fall off that porch, did you? Is that what this is all about? Some fireworks went off, you lost your balance and fell off that damn old porch?"

*   *   *

Momma is out of the room wheeled away and taken downstairs to another floor for a CAT scan. You'd had a CAT scan, too, but don't remember what it means: something to do with the skull, the brain.

Maybe the hemorrhages have ceased. Maybe the leaky blood has been reabsorbed by the brain. Maybe Momma will soon be well. You don't want to think beyond this, for now.

Another flower delivery is made for Teena Maguire. You will have it perched on her bedside tray when the nurses bring her back. Not a very big bouquet, one of the smaller, cheaper ones. But it's pretty: pink, red, white carnations and spiky green leaves. When Momma returns you show her the card, excited.

Hoping you will be well soon Teena.
Your friend J. Dromoor

But Momma is squinting, can't see to read. And she's confused, suspicious. When you tell her the name is "Dromoor" she says she has no friend by that name. She says, her voice rising, "I don't want anybody's damn pity, Bethie. *Tell them that.*"

Two NFPD detectives come to the room. Promise not to stay long. Not to tire or upset the patient. Just a few questions to ask. A few pictures of "suspects" for her to look at.

By this time, arrests have been made. Charges filed. Bail has been set at $75,000 for each of eight young men in custody.

*　　*　　*

By her twelfth day in St. Mary's, Teena Maguire is beginning to remember something of what happened to her. You see the stricken look in her face sometimes, her mouth opening in a silent cry. She knows now that it wasn't a car crash. It wasn't an accident. She knows that you were involved but that you weren't hurt as badly as she was. She knows that it happened on the Fourth of July, in the park. She has heard the word *assault*. It's possible that, given the nature of her injuries, she is thinking *rape*. Yet her knowledge is vague. She is so hopeful, trusting. The detectives speak patiently with her as you might speak with a frightened child. "I don't kn-know," she murmurs, beginning to tremble. "I'm afraid *I just don't know*." They have no luck showing her photographs of the suspects, for her bloodshot eyes fill so rapidly with tears, Teena is virtually blinded.

And so tired! In the midst of the interview with these awkward strangers, Teena Maguire falls asleep.

In the corridor your grandmother demands to know when *those animals* will be sent to prison.

The vigil at St. Mary's. The end of your childhood.

Naps. Meals on trays. Afternoon TV. Now that your mother can manage soft-solid foods, her appetite is returning. The gauze has been removed from her head, her scalp is tender, pinkish-pale, near-bald, but covered in soft, fair down like the down of a fledgling bird. At last Momma is free of the damn bedpan she'd hated, makes her slow shaky determined way to the lavatory leaning heavily on you and pulling the IV gurney. She jokes about slipping out of the hospital like this, running away home.

Home! What was Momma thinking?

Long days ebbing into dusk, and into night. The routines of a hospital. Routines of convalescence. Each night at 11:00 P.M., you and your grandmother leave your mother's room, Momma is already asleep. Wave good night to the nurses on the floor who smile at you, think you are a brave girl as your mother is a brave woman, fighting for her life and fighting now to recover. You would not wish to think for a fraction of a second that anyone at St. Mary's—nursing staff, aides and attendants and custodians, gift shop sales-clerks, cafeteria workers, the heavily made-up receptionist at the information desk—would not like you, would wish you harm.

Relatives of the suspects. Friends, neighbors.

Girlfriends.

That woman. What did she expect? Asking for it, the bitch.

Dressed like a hooker. Her word against theirs.

Who knows what was going on in that park in the middle of the night?!

You've seen the eyes. Drifting onto you and your grandmother Agnes Kevecki. You've seen, and looked quickly away.

Grandma doesn't seem to notice. Not Grandma! She's convinced that all of Niagara Falls is on her side, wanting *those animals* to be put away for a long time.

In the elevator the panic hits you, each night. Leaving your mother's room. The safety of that room. The vigil. Staring at the lighted numerals above the door moving swiftly from right to left flashing the floors as you descend to the ground floor. That sick-collapsing sensation in your stomach as the elevator door glides soundlessly open.

"Grandma. I'm so scared."

Grandma doesn't hear you. Lost in her own thoughts.

The enemy. Waiting for you. When you leave the hospital, when you return to the house on Baltic Avenue. For of course they know where you live. They know where your mother Teena Maguire lives: the rented duplex on Ninth.

They know all about Teena Maguire. The Picks, the Haabers, the DeLuccas, the Rickerts. These are East Side families, with numerous relatives. There are more of them than there are Keveckis and Maguires. Many more.

The Family Services woman says please don't worry.

The detectives say trust us. Don't worry.

There is a hearing scheduled for next month. (Though it will be postponed. You will come to learn that anything connected with the court, the law, legal issues, lawyers will be postponed. And postponed.) A hearing is not a trial but the preparation for a trial. You will be required to answer questions in court though you have already answered these questions many times. You have told, retold, and retold all that you can remember until you are sick with the telling as you are sick with the memory of what you must tell and retell to strangers who seem always to be doubting you, frowning and staring at you, assessing the validity of Bethel Maguire's testimony.

If Teena Maguire is well enough, she will be required to answer questions at the hearing. Your mother's testimony is more crucial than yours, the detectives have told you. Without her testimony, the case against the suspects will be circumstantial, weak.

You don't know why. You don't understand why this is so. They hurt your mother so badly, beat her and tore her insides and left her to bleed to death on the boathouse floor.

Yes but this has to be proven. In a court of law.

Not enough that it happened. That Teena Maguire almost died. It has to be proven, too.

"Grandma, I'm scared. . . ."

"Of what, honey? The parking garage? My car is parked right where we can see it. We got here so early."

Grandma loves you, but Grandma can't protect you. For how can Grandma protect you? She lives alone, an aging woman not in the very best of health herself, in her red-brick house on Baltic Avenue, a five-minute drive from the Twelfth Street/Huron Avenue neighborhood where the suspects and their families live. The "suspects"—as they are called—have been warned by police not to approach either your grandmother's house or your mother's house and not to approach anyone in your family at any time nor to attempt to contact anyone in your family and yet: they are the enemy, they are free on bail, they would wish to silence you. You know what they are. You remember them from the attack. Rushing at you, jeering and laughing. A wild-dog pack. Glistening eyes, teeth. *Fuck we should've killed them both, those cunts. When we had the fucking chance.*

The plan is that, when your mother is discharged from St. Mary's, she will come to live with Grandma, where you are living now. She will hire a nurse's aide to help with Momma for as long as necessary. And a physical therapist will come to the house several times a week, to help Momma walk again. Grandma has been a widow for twelve years and she has learned to cope with what she calls the inescapable facts of life and so she does not foresee trouble: *those animals* are guilty, *justice will be done,* they will tried, convicted, sentenced to prison *for a long time.* Grandma has uttered these words so frequently and so vehemently, to so many people, for her they have the ring of prophecy.

When you're with Grandma, you try to believe.

Insult

RAY CASEY WAS DRINKING. Dropping by taverns on Huron Avenue. It would be said the poor bastard had gone looking for a fight.

Since *what-happened-to-Teena,* Casey had been having a hard time. Hard to tell Teena he loved her, hard to be in the same room with Teena. If he touched her he'd hurt her. He knew she wanted to be comforted, and he wanted to comfort her. But it scared him to touch her, not knowing if she'd wince, or try not to wince, smile at him this forced stiff smile so he knew he was hurting her, so clumsy. He'd bought her bright pretty silk scarfs for her poor baldy head Teena called it she didn't want to show, till her hair grew out better. Bought her a fruit basket, flowers. But Casey had his own family down in Corning. Telephone calls! Had to deal with his kids' crazy mother. Had to deal with three kids going through teenage crises of their own. His sixteen-year-old daughter cutting herself, threatening to kill herself. Had to pay fucking bills. Had to deal with his fucking boss. Had to deal with people in the neighborhood looking at him. At Ray Casey whose woman friend Teena Maguire had been gang-raped in Rocky Point Park.

Hard to know what to do. Every fucking waking moment of Ray Casey's life trying to know what to do.

So he went drinking on Huron Avenue. By himself. Mack's Tavern, where the Picks and their friends hung out. Got into a fight one Friday day night not with either of the Picks, not with any of the suspects but with a guy named Thurles, cousin of the Picks, Casey swung at him first and broke his nose and there was a fistfight raw and clumsy and both men were bleeding within seconds and somebody calls the cops, and these two uniforms break it up and everybody at the bar reports it was Casey who started the fight, came into Mack's already drunk and looking for trouble. In the patrol car, the younger cop asks Casey is this about Teena Maguire and Casey can't answer at first. Casey is wiping his bloodied mouth on some wadded tissue the cops have given him. The younger cop asks again very carefully enunciating *Teen-a Ma-guire* and Casey says yeah maybe. Maybe it is about her. And the younger cop says, "You don't want to do this. This is a mistaken thing you are doing. Where there's witnesses." The older cop is sympathetic with Casey, too, but says they have to bring him in anyway. The younger cop says, "Why?"

"Why"

ONE DAY SHE KNEW. One hour.

Must've been a window open. And something flew in, frenzied wings beating at her face.

She remembered then. Not all of it, but enough.

Through the walls of several rooms in Grandma's house you heard her cry out as if she'd been hit another time.

The week following the discharge from the hospital. A few days after Casey showed up, face swollen like raw meat and trying to make a joke of it, he'd walked into a fucking door. And the fat-girl therapist acting weird with Teena, not friendly like you would expect, not like the nurses at St. Mary's but strangely sullen, and hurting Teena massaging her atrophied muscles as if Teena deserved to be punished, letting herself go.

You ran into the room. There was Momma who'd been walking with her cane, now sitting on the edge of a chair rocking slowly back and forth pressing her fists into her eyes. You saw now clearly that Teena Maguire was no longer a woman whom other women envied, or glanced at in interest and admiration out on the street. You saw that she did not want you to come near her, to touch her.

"Why? Why would they want to hurt *me?*"

"Bitch You Better"

*BITCH YOU BETTER BE SAYING YOUR PRAYS
WHOR BETTER BE ON YOUR KNEES NOT
SUCKING COCKS*

This scrawled message in tarry black letters on a piece of dirty cardboard Teena Maguire found propped against the side door of her mother's house on Baltic Avenue, three days before the hearing.

Since the rape, Teena's vision wasn't always reliable. In good light she could see about as well as before but if the light was hazy or occluded or if, as in this instance, she was taken by surprise, her eyes swam with tears. She stared at the message, read and reread it and tried to comprehend it. The hatred emanating from it.

She folded the stiff cardboard in two. She stuffed it into one of the plastic trash cans at the side of the house. She would say nothing about it to anyone wishing to think possibly it had been a mistake, a message meant for some other woman in some other house on Baltic Avenue.

Secrets

Iɴ ᴛʜᴇ 7-Eʟᴇᴠᴇɴ ʏᴏᴜ saw them. Their eyes moving on you.
" 'Bethel Maguire.' You're *her*?"

They stared at you unsmiling. Your name was uttered in
contempt.

The largest girl, in sweatshirt and jeans and boy's sneakers,
advanced upon you, pushing your shoulder with the flat of
her hand.

"See, you better watch your mouth, bitch. You better not
be saying wrong things about my brothers, bitch. 'Cause
what they begun out there in the park, see, they're gonna
finish up, you and your bitch momma don't keep your
fucking mouths shut."

Grandma's long-haired orange cat Tigerlily. She'd been
missing for three days. You searched for her in the neighborhood, knocked at doors. Grandma was so upset, you'd never
seen Grandma so upset. Grandma stood on the porch calling
Kitty-kitty-kitty-kitty! in a forlorn-hopeful voice.

You didn't wish to think that Tigerlily had been taken.

You wished to think that Tigerlily had wandered off. You wished to think that, if Tigerlily had been struck by a car and crawled away to die, it was only a coincidence, the hearing scheduled for later this week.

Finally you found the cat's stiffened body, in the alley behind Baltic Avenue. Three houses down from Grandma's. Her tawny yellow eyes were open and blank. Her white whiskers were stiff with blood. The full, fluffy ruff around her neck you had loved to stroke was stiff with blood. You could not determine how Tigerlily had died, how they had killed her. Maybe with a rock. Or maybe one of them had kicked her to death. She had not been a large cat, a few blows would have killed her.

You recalled your mother's baffled cry.

"Why? Why would they want to hurt *me?*"

You began to cry, carrying Tigerlily in your arms. You would bury her in the backyard, in secret. You would not tell Grandma, who would continue to call *Kitty-kitty!* from the porch for another day or so.

The Hearing: September 1996

"Shit."

Dromoor knew it would be bad. His gut instinct was to wish to hell he had no part in it.

He saw who the lead defense attorney was. He knew the man's reputation in Niagara Falls and Buffalo, too.

He saw the mostly hostile crowd pushing into the courtroom, filling every available seat by 8:40 A.M. And this a weekday.

He saw the defendants. All were clean-shaven. The one whose parole had been revoked wore an orange prison jumpsuit stamped with OLEAN MEN'S FACILITY that gave him a look of clownish formality. The others were neatly dressed in suits, shirts, neckties, polished shoes. They'd had haircuts. Their tattoos were hidden. Even the coarse-faced Picks bore only a cursory resemblance to the punks taken into police custody on the morning of July 5.

He saw the woman Teena Maguire. And her daughter, Bethel.

The prosecution's chief witnesses: the victims.

Teena Maguire was wearing dark glasses that suggested an incongruous glamour in this staid setting and she was wearing a floral print silk scarf tied about her head that suggested childlike innocence, frivolity. She was heavily made up to disguise her scarred face. Her mouth was crimson as a blood clot. The female deputy prosecutor who would argue the case had probably advised her to wear conservative clothes, and so Teena Maguire was wearing a navy blue sheath with a small prim jacket that fitted her loosely, a white silk blouse beneath. She wore low-heeled shoes. She entered the room hesitantly and stiffly like a blind woman being led onto thin ice. She was leaning against her daughter who was looking older than Dromoor recalled as if in the scant nine weeks since July Fourth the girl had rapidly and unnaturally matured. Teena Maguire's expression was vague and dazed and she may have been smiling faintly. She stumbled once or twice, the deputy prosecutor quickly took her arm. She seemed to see no one, not even the prosecutor, who was speaking urgently to her. She took no evident notice of the numerous young men at the defense table who were staring at her with undisguised resentment, hatred. Initially she took no notice of an agitated middle-aged woman in the first row of spectators, mother of the defendants Marvin and Lloyd Pick, who was flush-faced in indignation mouthing just-audible words in Teena Maguire's direction: "Bitch! Whore! Liar!"

Bailiffs advanced swiftly upon the woman to threaten her with expulsion. It wasn't clear at first whether she would desist, other family members were trying to calm her, angrily she shook off a restraining arm and cursed the bailiffs in a furious undertone and in virtually the same moment she was helped to her feet, urged out into the aisle as a stout younger woman, clearly a relative, pushed her way out to join her, shouting, "They didn't do it! You got the wrong parties! This is a fucking setup! This is the Gestapo!" as the bailiffs led her away.

Beside Dromoor, Zwaaf shifted in his seat. "Fucking Jesus. This ain't even the trial."

Look: don't get involved. Whatever shit happens to these people isn't happening to you.

It was too late, though. Since he'd first seen the dazed bloodied girl at the side of the roadway in Rocky Point Park, and since he'd first seen the woman broken and bloodied on the filthy boathouse floor, it had been too late for him.

"All rise."

The judge entered the courtroom. He was breathing quickly, as if he'd been running. He, too, was flush-faced in indignation, he'd been informed of the commotion in his courtroom but would not acknowledge it.

Schpiro was the judge's name. He was in his midfifties, short, with sharp-glinting wire-rimmed eyeglasses. In his pompous black robe he looked squat as a fire hydrant. Except that Schpiro was a judge presiding over a courtroom with the power to irrevocably alter lives, he would not have merited a second glance from anyone in the courtroom. The peevish bulldog set of his mouth indicated that he was aware of this fact and he would tolerate no bullshit in his courtroom. He was a politician, canny. He knew the volatile nature of the case he was assigned to adjudicate and he would make no mistakes if he could avoid them. Dromoor saw that Schpiro recognized on sight every attorney in the room: prosecution, defense. Except for the deputy prosecutor sitting beside Teena Maguire, all were men. Schpiro exchanged a nod of greeting with only one of these, the lead defense attorney Kirkpatrick. Neither man smiled. But Dromoor saw the look that passed between them, of subtle acknowledgment, respect. Thinking *Fuckers. Probably belong to the same yacht club.*

The lead deputy prosecutor Diebenkorn rose to address Judge Schpiro. Her manner was deferential, guarded. She was a woman of indeterminate age: not young, not yet middle-aged. When she spoke too rapidly out of nervousness, Schpiro told her, "Hold your horses, counselor," and there was a mild titter from the rows of spectators. Dromoor thought this was a bad sign: Schpiro playing to the crowd. Diebenkorn was a natural foil. She was earnest, righteous. She wore a charcoal gray pants suit with wide trouser legs in an outmoded style. Her hair was a brown frizz-perm. It was her duty to outline the state's case against the numerous defendants naming them individually, specifying charges in her flat nasal upstate voice. This would be a complicated case involving a complicated legal procedure. Dromoor wondered why the state was requesting a single trial, with a single jury. There were eyewitness testimonies from the two victims linking just five of the defendants to the crime. There were DNA and other forensic evidence linking these defendants and three others to the crime. A ninth defendant, not present at this hearing, had confessed to his role in the crime and would be a state's witness against the others; a transcript of his testimony would be presented to Schpiro. Diebenkorn argued that the crime had been an especially vicious sexual attack—a "gang rape." It had been an attack against a woman in the presence of her twelve-year-old daughter who had also been assaulted and threatened with rape. It had been a prolonged attack, lasting nearly half an hour. It had been a premeditated attack for the rapists had stalked their victims in Rocky Point Park for an estimated ten minutes, according to the testimony of the state's witness. It had been an attack intended to result in the death of Martine Maguire, who had been left to bleed to death, unconscious on the floor of a boathouse in a secluded area of the park. If Mrs. Maguire's daughter Bethel had not been present, terrified and hiding in a corner of the boathouse, Martine Maguire would not be alive today to confront and give testimony against her attackers. As it was, Mrs. Maguire had suffered critical physical injuries, had been on life support at St. Mary's Hospital and subsequently hospitalized for several weeks, and at the present time was still recuperating from the attack. "Your Honor, Mrs. Maguire's presence in the courtroom today is something of a miracle."

Dromoor had been watching Teena Maguire and saw her stiffen. Must be hell to hear yourself talked of like that. Gang rape, bleed to death, left to die. This was ugly.

Beside Teena Maguire, the daughter. Dromoor had a daughter of his own now, two years old. Jesus! He could not bear to think of it, he would murder with his bare hands anyone who even threatened to hurt her.

He hoped to hell the prosecution could strike plea bargains with those bastards, to avoid a trial. They could not seriously expect Bethel Maguire to testify in court. To endure cross-examinations from defense lawyers like the jackal Kirkpatrick.

He saw the girl looking toward him. Dark startled eyes. He wondered if she remembered him.

Dromoor recalled how he'd first seen Bethel Maguire, by the roadway in Rocky Point Park. Disheveled, bloodied. Her clothes torn. He'd been sick to think that the girl had been raped. She'd looked at him with such desperate hope. As if he, a police officer out on routine patrol, dispatched by chance to the scene of a crime, had the power to truly help her.

My mother is hurt! Please help her! I'm afraid my mother is dying please please help her!

In that instant, Dromoor was pulled in.

As if their lives had gotten tangled with his, Christ knows why.

Like tangled fishing lines. Knotted together.

Dromoor had seen a lot of things. Ugly things. He'd done some ugly things himself. Things you'd imagine you would not forget, but he'd forgotten. Except this girl Bethel, and her mother, Teena, in the boathouse.

* * *

The hearing proceeded. There were numerous interruptions. A lawyer is basically a mouth, like a shark is a mouth attached to a long gut. The business of lawyers is to talk, to interrupt one another, and to devour one another if possible. Dromoor who hated court appearances like any other cop had only just been sworn in and begun his brief testimony reciting the facts of his involvement at the crime scene when he was interrupted by Schpiro's dry voice: "Officer. Excuse me."

Dromoor must have stared blankly at the judge, there was a titter in the courtroom.

" 'My partner and *I*,' Officer. Not 'My partner and *me*.' "

Dromoor knew that he was expected to reply. He was expected to say something conciliatory that would include the words *Your Honor*. But he did not.

Schpiro said, with an air of leaden patience, "Officer, continue. 'My partner and *I*.' "

So Dromoor knew from the start it would go badly for the prosecution.

In her flat earnest nasal voice Diebenkorn presented the state's case in outline. It soon developed that she had a verbal tic of saying "Your Honor" to which Schpiro politely responded, "I am here" or "Yes. I am listening." The judge's air of scarcely concealed impatience made the female prosecutor ever more nervous. She paused to sort through files, documents. She conferred with her colleagues. There was a good deal of testimony regarding DNA and forensic evidence, for while there was such evidence linking several of the defendants to the rape, evidence was not yet available or missing in other instances; where there was eyewitness testimony, there was not invariably forensic evidence. The case would be partially circumstantial. Each of the defendants presented an individual problem. Only one of the arrested men had confessed, and he had confessed only to assault, not aggravated assault and not rape. He had named others in the rape but had spared himself. Lawyers for the defendants were challenging his testimony, claiming that he lied in exchange for lesser charges; he had a prison record, and would make a poor prosecutorial witness. And there was the matter of other individuals involved in the rape/assault who had not yet been named and apprehended. Dryly Schpiro said, "In the event of a trial, the state will present its case more thoroughly, I assume?"

Chastened, Diebenkorn murmured, "Yes, Your Honor."

Ordinarily by this time Dromoor would have slipped from the courtroom. His partner Zwaaf had departed. But something held Dromoor there, a morbid curiosity and dread as of one about to witness a train derailment.

"Mrs. Maguire. It is not bright sunshine here, you might remove your dark glasses."

Schpiro spoke politely yet with an air of impatience. He was a judge keenly alert to frivolity in his courtroom. The dark glasses with their pathos of glamour, the floral print scarf tied about the woman's head to disguise her sparse tufted hair, annoyed him.

Teena Maguire fumbled to remove the glasses, and dropped them. Diebenkorn, breathing through her mouth, stooped to retrieve them as they clattered to the floor. She explained to Schpiro that since her injuries, Mrs. Maguire's eyes were unusually sensitive to light. Schpiro expressed some measured sympathy, saying that Mrs. Maguire might partially close her eyes. Teena spoke slowly and haltingly and not very coherently as Diebenkorn led her through an abbreviated testimony. It was clear that Teena had suffered neurological damage; often she paused for several seconds to search for the correct word. She had recovered only partial memory of the rape/assault. She had been able to positively identify only three of the rapists. When Diebenkorn asked if these individuals were present in the courtroom, Teena could not at first reply. She hid her face in her hands. She wiped at her eyes. Almost inaudibly she murmured yes. But asked to point them out, she hesitated for a long moment before concurring with the request.

With a shaking hand Teena pointed out Marvin Pick, Lloyd Pick, and Jimmy DeLucca, who were sitting immobile at the defense table staring frozen-faced at her. At the precinct, she had picked out Haaber instead of DeLucca. Partly the confusion had to do with the young men's similar haircuts and clothing. Their lawyers had instructed them to look as much like one another as possible. Haaber had had a small mustache at the time of the rape, his hair had been much longer. Teena seemed to realize her mistake, there was an immediate buzz of indignation from the spectators, but she could not stammer out the words to rectify it.

The daughter, Bethel, spoke more clearly. But she was visibly trembling. Staring at Diebenkorn as if terrified of looking elsewhere. From time to time Schpiro interrupted to ask Bethel to speak louder, but the judge was not sarcastic with her. He would not wish to appear unsympathetic with a child victim of a violent sexual attack, at least at the preliminary hearing.

Kirkpatrick addressed Judge Schpiro.

The defense's rebuttal of the charges against the defendants was a simple one: there had been no rape.

No rape! None.

Admittedly there had been sex. Multiple acts of sex. But the sex had been entirely consensual. Martine Maguire had known each of the defendants and was "well known" by them. The sex had been for money and the deal had gone wrong (Maguire had wanted more money than she'd been promised, or the young men had less to give her, this part of the disagreement was unclear), and the alleged victim, who had been drinking at the time, became verbally and then physically aggressive against her young clients. The young men, admittedly under the influence of alcohol and controlled substances, had fought back when she attacked them, but had not hurt her seriously; they had left the boathouse, and other, unidentified young men had entered, drawn by the commotion. The severe beating and instances of rape must have happened at that time.

"Those assailants, the NFPD has yet to identify and arrest."

As for Maguire's daughter who had allegedly hidden in a corner of the boathouse at the time of her mother's sexual encounters—"My clients and their companions were entirely unaware of her presence. They certainly had no knowledge of a twelve-year-old girl! Apparently the girl hurt herself crawling in the storage area. In her testimony she admits that she did not 'actively see' any acts of rape, only just heard them, or believed that she heard them. This was a confused, frightened child whose mother was so derelict as a parent she'd brought the child to a wild, drunken orgy of a Fourth of July party, and afterward led her into Rocky Point Park at midnight, to meet up with young men from the neighborhood whom she knew well, and whom she boldly propositioned for sex. The girl is a victim, yes: a victim of her mother's outrageous negligence. She was confused at the time of the alleged rape and may have been purposefully misled by Maguire at a later time. Her testimony, like her mother's, is entirely fabricated and misleading. As the evidence and my clients' testimonies will show—"

There was an air of shock in the courtroom. Delayed shock, as in the aftermath of a sonic boom.

Then, from the rows of spectators, exclamations and scattered applause. Schpiro was as much taken by surprise as anyone and did not strike his gavel for several seconds, when it appeared that things might swerve out of control. "Quiet! Or I will clear the courtroom!"

Teena Maguire was protesting, incredulous. Diebenkorn tried to quiet her. There were raised voices from the spectators in the first several rows. Some of these were sympathetic with Teena Maguire, and furious on her account; others were hostile to her, and gloating. Individuals were on their feet.

Diebenkorn and another deputy prosecutor were helping Teena Maguire as if she'd begun to fall, or to struggle. Bailiffs and guards charged forward. Schpiro was obliged to clear his courtroom after all: flush-faced, indignant, striking his gavel even as his words—"Enough! Enough!"—went unheard. On the evening news it would be reported *The atmosphere quickly became too unruly for the judge to control.*

Dromoor had seen the derailment. Sick in the gut, had to escape.

Part II

Wind Drives Us Crazy

At the Falls she leaned over the railing. The wind blew cold spray into her face, clothes. Within seconds her clothes were soaked and clung to her thin body. Tourists perceived her as a drunk or drugged or deranged woman and kept their distance from her. On her head she wore a silk scarf that loosened in the wind, slipped from her head, and was blown out above the thunderous water; without the scarf, her hair was revealed as sparse, tufted, without color. Now she was perceived as possibly a sick woman, one who has lost her hair to chemotherapy.

Her face was a chalky-white face that looked as if, mask-like, it might be torn from her too, to be blown away into the frothy water.

Genius!

The woman's word against theirs. Anybody can cry rape. Reasonable doubt is all a jury needs. Who can prove, disprove? Kirkpatrick is a genius, isn't he? Best damn criminal lawyer in upstate New York. Of course you'll have to refinance your home, sell your second car. Beg borrow steal, the guy isn't cheap. But just the man to call when you're in deep deep shit.

The Broken Woman

It was the end for Teena Maguire in Niagara Falls, she could not bear it. Never would she testify now. Never would she reenter any courtroom. No faith in any fucking courtroom! No faith in any fucking prosecutors, judges. Serve her a subpoena, threaten her with contempt of court *she would not*.

After the hearing that day she'd collapsed and had had to be hospitalized again for shock, exhaustion. She was diagnosed as anemic. She was diagnosed as severely depressed. She was diagnosed as suicidal. She was put on a regimen of antidepressant medication, which after a few weeks, she refused to take. She began seeing psychotherapists, rape counselors, but soon ceased. She was too tired to get out of bed in the morning. She was too tired to shower, shampoo her hair. She would not see women friends she'd known since high school. She'd ceased even to speak with Ray Casey on the phone. Often she refused to see her own mother in whose house on Baltic Avenue she was living.

Often she refused to see you.

*   *   *

*Leave me alone can't you for Christ's sake. I'm sick. I'm so tired. I
can't give a damn about you or anybody else.*

Teena Maguire claimed she could not remember what had
happened to her in Rocky Point Park in July, or in the Niagara County Courthouse in September. She'd been pretty
much beat up each time. Could not remember faces, couldn't
identify. Could not remember names. It hurt her head to try
to think. She was giving it all up, she made no effort to
remember. *Teena's pathetic. Worthless. Piece of shit. Who gives a
damn about Teena she's a fucking joke huh?*

Sometimes she took the damn medication, more often
not. Make her sick. Constipated. Head-not-right. Better to
drop by the package store around the corner and buy a
six-pack of beer, a bottle of cheap Italian red wine. Couldn't
afford good whiskey, not Teena! The dentist-brothers had
hired another receptionist. They'd given her three months'
salary, she'd be eligible for unemployment. If she could force
herself to go downtown and apply. Of course, she'd given
up the row house on Ninth Street. She'd moved back with
her mother. If she tried, she might get men to buy drinks
for her, in which case she could drink reasonably good
whiskey, bourbon, vodka, but it was not worth it for her
to listen to the men, to smell the men, and to see their
faces in whatever haze of drunkenness their faces floated
in at the periphery of her wavering vision. Nor could she
bear to be touched by any man. No, no! God, no. Pan-

icked, screamed, scratched at them, disturbed other patrons and so she was not welcome in these bars in which in any case she had no desire to go. Better for Teena Maguire to buy her own provisions. Keep to herself. Walk the windy bluff at the edge of the Falls where it was always damp with spray. In fair weather the area swarmed with tourists like ants but in bad weather she was likely to be alone. Leaning against the railing above the American Falls. Staring into the crazed churning water far below.

At the Whirlpool just below the Falls, sixty-foot vertical walls of water rushed in a giant circle fasterfasterfaster as if about to disappear into a giant drain.

God help me. God give me peace. God?

"Ma'am! You don't want to do that, ma'am."

Whoever it was interrupting her reverie, sometimes daring to take her arm, Teena was indifferent. She shrugged, she made no reply. Often she was driven home by park officials/NFPD officers soaked through, shivering convulsively and her teeth chattering yet with a curious passivity, as if by being taking into custody in such a way she'd become again merely a body, an inert and soulless weight.

Her hair had grown back grudgingly, lank and curiously without color. When she saw her reflection in a mirror, taken unawares she did not think alarmed *I must do something about my appearance, Jesus!* but *That pathetic woman, they should have finished the job.*

*   *   *

One evening in early October it was Dromoor who brought Teena home.

You saw from your window upstairs at the front of your grandmother's house. Saw the unfamiliar vehicle, a Ford station wagon, low-slung and not new, the kind you'd expect to see littered with kids' toys in the backseat, pull up to the curb. And out of the driver's seat a tall man in a dark canvas jacket, bareheaded, with a shaved-looking steely-glinting head, going around to help your mother out of the passenger's seat. Teena lurched to her feet, leaning against the man's arm even as she made an effort to stand on her own.

At first you didn't recognize John Dromoor, out of uniform. Then you did.

You ran downstairs breathless. "Momma?"—you called out. Pretending not to know who was with you, bringing Teena home.

She'd been drinking again. And she was sick. She refused to take medication, see her therapist. Didn't seem to give a damn what happened to her any longer.

You halted at the foot of the stairs. Saw them just inside the front door, in the outer vestibule. Through the frosted-glass doors you could not hear what they were saying. Mostly Dromoor spoke. But what was he saying? How well did they know each other? They were not touching. You could hear Dromoor's voice—low, urgent, almost eager—but not his words.

Your mother laughed suddenly, without mirth. A shrill sound like glass breaking.

Pushing then through the swinging doors into the inner vestibule, not seeming to see you; or, seeing you, paying no heed. Behind her Dromoor hesitated, as if wanting to follow her. But better not.

He saw you then. He wasn't smiling. He knew you of course—since the roadway in Rocky Point Park, he knew you—but had never yet called you by name.

Awkwardly you pushed through the frosted-glass doors. You were a shy girl made bold, brazen. Your heart rang like a deranged bell in your chest. You were breathless stammering, "M-Mister Dromoor?—thank you for bringing Momma home."

Dromoor must have known, at that moment. The look in your face. The heat in your face. Yearning, desperation.

I love you. You are all to me.

You would remember: Dromoor telling you this was a hard time for your mother, you would have to take care of her. And you said, too quickly, in a voice of childish hurt, "I don't think my mother wants anybody to take care of her."

Alone with Dromoor in the vestibule of your grandmother's house. A roaring in your ears, as if you were leaning over a railing at the Falls: the visceral wallop of infatuation, the most powerful emotion you'd ever experienced in your life.

Dromoor frowned at your words. He'd chosen his own with such care.

Dromoor left his cell phone number neatly written on a piece of paper. To pass on to Teena. Beneath the number these words:

Any hour of the day or night.

D

The Female Prosecutor

GODDAMN HE'D ENTERED HER dreams. So shameful.

She could not control it! Could not control the case! The most highly publicized criminal trial in years in Niagara Falls and Harriet Diebenkorn's opportunity at long-delayed last to prove herself to her skeptical male elders and she was publicly humiliated at the hearing, bushwacked. Never saw it coming. No more than the rape victim had seen it coming.

Kirkpatrick, Jay. He was Diebenkorn's new nemesis. She was a woman who swerved from obsession to obsession and most of them male but none of them quite like Jay Kirkpatrick that bastard. Obsessed with Kirkpatrick. No wonder the man's reputation! She'd been only vaguely aware now she was well aware. Rising to his feet and with an air of courteous and even gentlemanly regret riddling the state's case with *reasonable doubt* as the most finished-appearing wood might be riddled from within by termites. Bastard never raised his voice. He was one to provoke others to raise their voices. He was not a handsome man, his skin was actually rather coarse and his pitiless eyes close-set on either side of his beak of a nose, and yet he exuded the air of a handsome man, suave and self-assured. Kirkpatrick had a cowboy swagger, though he wore custom-made pinstripe suits and muted Italian ties. His vanity was highly polished black leather shoe boots with pointed toes and inch-high heels. You expected Kirk-patrick, scoring another of his devastating points in court, to execute a staccato dance step with those heels.

"Jay Kirkpatrick." You had to smile, shake your head over him.

Kirkpatrick had made his reputation in the Buffalo area in 1989. Brilliantly defended the twenty-one-year-old druggie son of a wealthy Buffalo manufacturer who had shot and killed his father. The plea was not guilty for reason of self-defense. Though the father had been unarmed, near-naked, climbing up dripping wet from his swimming pool in the leafy affluent suburb of Amherst, and the son had fired six bullets into his body from a distance of eight feet. Yet Kirkpatrick had convinced a credulous jury that the son had been in "immediate, overwhelming" fear of his life.

Yes. You had to smile. Kirkpatrick was a sly one.

Diebenkorn hated it, Kirkpatrick had entered her dreams. Probably as powerfully, Diebenkorn was prone to think, as that dog-pack of loser punks had entered the dreams of pathetic broken Martine Maguire.

The first time Diebenkorn came to the house on Baltic Avenue to speak with the gang-rape victim, Teena Maguire would not see her. Sick with a headache, Teena had been in bed all the previous day. Too exhausted to lift her head from the pillow. Teena's grim-faced mother, Agnes Kevecki, grudgingly allowed Diebenkorn to enter her house, asking her to wipe her feet on the doormat first. As Diebenkorn uttered her prepared breathy speech *I must see her. I am a deputy prosecutor with the county district attorney's office and I insist upon seeing Martine Maguire* the older woman said bluntly it was so, her daughter Martine was not a well woman any longer. "Not in her body, and not in her mind. Not just those animals but you people at the courthouse have destroyed her."

The Diebenkorn woman, as your grandmother would refer to her afterward, leaned forward breathing through her mouth so humid you could almost see it in the air like steam: "Mrs. Kevecki! What a thing to say! The county attorney's office is committed to seeking justice for your daughter and granddaughter, we intend through the law to make restitution to them for the suffering they have experienced! But we must have their cooperation as witnesses. Martine has said she is dropping charges. And will not allow her daughter to testify. But they can't refuse to help us now. If—"

Your grandmother stood with her arms tightly folded across her sloping shelf of a bust. Her steely-ivory hair fitted her skull like a sleek cap and her skin looked as if it had been squeezed in a powerful hand, and released in a pattern of fine wrinkles. She said, with an air of infinite contempt, "You! 'Prosecutors.' You promised to protect my daughter. And you did not."

"Mrs. Kevecki, we could not anticipate—"

"You must be ignorant, then. You must be inexperienced. We can't trust you."

"But Mrs. Kevecki—"

"That man, calling my daughter a whore! A hooker! My poor daughter who was almost killed! Exposing her to such shame! You allowed it, you did not prevent it. A trial would kill her. A trial would kill all of us. Every day in the newspapers, on TV—it would kill our family. And you dare to suggest that my granddaughter be exposed, too!"

Diebenkorn protested, "The defense counsel is unscrupulous! Kirkpatrick is a—a notorious distorter of truths. The man turns truth upside down. Inside out. He's a black magician. He should be disbarred. He resorts to such vicious tactics because he knows that the case against his clients is overwhelming. And a jury will know, I promise! I will see to it, Mrs. Kevecki, I promise. But your daughter and granddaughter, Mrs. Kevecki, must—"

Your grandmother rose stiffly. Her heart fluttered when she was becoming upset. A daily handful of white and green pills monitored her blood pressure yet even so at such moments a pulse beat heavily in her head.

"Ms. Diebehkorn, there is no 'must' in this house for my daughter and my granddaughter. Good-bye."

The second time Diebenkorn came to the house on Baltic Avenue, your grandmother refused to answer the door. You slipped out to speak to the prosecutor on the front porch.

It was a damp, overcast day at the Falls. Sky like a dirty bandage and wind from the river smelling like wet chalk.

Diebenkorn began by apologizing profusely. She'd been

taken by surprise by Kirkpatrick. Bushwacked! Her entire team! That would not happen again, Diebenkorn promised.

"Everybody in Niagara Falls knows that the rapists and their attorneys are lying. Absolute lies! The entire story is concocted, an invention of Jay Kirkpatrick. The defendants originally told police, when they were brought into custody, that they didn't know Martine Maguire, had never seen or heard of Martine Maguire. They told police they'd never been in the park that night, which is a preposterous lie, we have a dozen witnesses who saw them. And now, this claim of . . ." Diebenkorn paused, panting. You could see the pupils of her eyes contracting. She was speaking to a thirteen-year-old girl, an assault victim. She was speaking to the daughter of a rape victim. Yet she had no choice but to continue, vehemently, like a runaway trailer-truck, ". . . 'consensual sex.' 'Sex for money.' Ridiculous! Any reasonable jury will reject it. I will see to it that they reject it. And the preposterous claim that a second pack of rapists rushed in—oh, impossible! How a defense attorney can argue such nonsense with a straight face, I don't know. Believe me, Bethel. And tell your mother."

Blankly you stared at Diebenkorn. You had a new habit of going empty-eyed and uncomprehending when it suited you. It would be a stratagem to serve you through years of public school in Niagara Falls at times in the very presence of enemies. You saw that Diebenkorn had smeared a dark crimson lipstick on her thin lips and that there was lipstick on her front teeth.

Diebenkorn said, guiltily, "It is true, I have to concede. Kirkpatrick has a staff of legal investigators whose mission it is to uncover dirt about the victims of his clients. His courtroom strategy is to attack the victim, in this case Martine Maguire, to make it appear that she brought her misfortune upon herself. Kirkpatrick believes that if a jury feels that a victim deserves her punishment, they will not wish to punish the defendant but will *identify with the defendant*. 'Juries want to vote not guilty, it's the generous Christian gesture.' " Diebenkorn laughed with a strange excitement.

She continued to plead. To threaten. (Just a little. Subpoena? Martine Maguire in her sickbed?) She promised that she and her team would not be "bushwacked" a second time. At the trial, they would have notification of the defense witnesses, they would know beforehand what lies, innuendo, slander were to be presented in court. They would have a chance to rebut. And the rape shield laws in New York State prevent certain kinds of disclosures, Schpiro would be forced to comply. And the forensic evidence—semen, blood, hair, fiber—was overwhelming. The testimonies of the victims, mother and daughter, would be damning. If Teena withdrew her cooperation, the rapists could plea bargain much lighter sentences than they deserved, and that would be *unjust*.

You told Diebenkorn you didn't guess that your mother would cooperate with her anymore. You didn't guess that your mother would give much of a damn about *unjust*.

"Bethel, my life is bound up with this case, too. It isn't just a 'case' to me it's—it has to do with my life as a woman, too—for when one woman is viciously attacked, the way your mother was, all women are being attacked. That's why rape must be punished as a serious, violent crime."

Diebenkorn paused, wiping at her eyes. She appeared to be deeply moved. "Bethel, will you at least ask Teena if I could speak with her? Just briefly, today? The defense senses our hesitation, Kirkpatrick is moving now for a 'swift trial.' I know that I have disappointed Teena, and others, but I promise that I will make up for it. Please give me a chance!"

You didn't think there was much hope but you were a good girl and invited Diebenkorn to step inside the vestibule while you ran upstairs. You hoped that Grandma wouldn't discover her and ask her to leave.

Upstairs you knocked softly on Momma's door. No answer.

She had not been out for several days. Not since John Dromoor had brought her home.

You knocked again on Momma's door. You opened it, to peer inside. The room was darkened, your nostrils pinched against a smell of slept-in bedclothes, perspiration. Momma was lying on top of her bed, on a rumpled quilt bedspread, bare-legged, in just her bathrobe, on her side, unmoving.

Momma don't die. Please Momma we saved you once don't die now.

Strange to see your own mother sleeping. Unaware, oblivious.

There was no black pool of blood beneath her. You could hear her breathing. A harsh rasping sound like fabric being torn. Yet Momma was peaceful-seeming, lying on her side as a child might lie with her hands clenched between drawn-up knees.

You did not speak. Your heart was beating quickly as if in the presence of danger.

Quietly you shut the door. If Momma could sleep, that was good. It was your duty to let her sleep.

In any case you knew how Teena Maguire felt about the rapists now. You'd heard her tell your grandmother why should she give a damn, let the fuckers rape other women. Nothing to do with her.

Downstairs, Diebenkorn waited eagerly. Those damp doggy eyes.

You hesitated. You bit your lower lip. It was a TV moment, or maybe a court-moment. It was not a rehearsed moment, not exactly.

"Oh gosh! Ms. Diebenkorn! I'm afraid all Momma says to say to you is," in a lowered voice, with a semblance of a blush, " 'fuck you.' "

"Self-Defense"

O N OCTOBER 11, 1996, Dromoor killed one of the rapists with two shots from his .45-caliber police service revolver.

You learned this news from Teena.

"The first of them. He's dead."

Teena spoke dazedly. Her eyes burned with fever.

The first of them. You would wonder if these were Dromoor's words, carefully chosen.

You would wonder if Dromoor had called Teena from the parking lot, on his cell phone. Except no, such a call might be traced. He would have waited, to call from a public phone some distance from the shooting. But he wouldn't have waited long.

Next you saw TV news. And next the *Niagara Journal*.

DeLucca, James. "Jimmy." Twenty-four, unemployed at the time of his death. Resident 1194 Forge Street, his parents' home in Niagara Falls. Survived by . . .

There was DeLucca on the TV screen. Photo taken when he'd been in a glittery doped-up mood. Greasy dark hair falling in his face. Presley/greaser style. Some girls would think he was sexy. An overgrown kid. This photo didn't show DeLucca as he'd looked in the courthouse in his neatly pressed serge suit and neatly tied necktie and neatly combed haircut but more the way he'd actually looked that night in Rocky Point Park. Careening into you. Whooping, yelping. One of the dog pack yipping as he'd leapt to block you with muscled arms outstretched like it's a rough basketball game, somebody has passed you the ball, you are vulnerable and trapped and the target and DeLucca is the guy laughing as he crashes into you.

Hey babygirl! Babygirl gonna show us your titties, too?

In the living room, blinds drawn. Turning from one TV channel to another to follow the news. Momma stares at the screen with her fever-eyes, hands clamped between her knees. Grandma watches murmuring to herself. And you.

Why two bullets? Where one would've been fatal?

Carefully it would be explained by NFPD spokesmen that two shots are a NFPD requirement. If an officer has made a decision that deadly force is necessary he is trained to fire two shots.

Dromoor was only following his NFPD training.

The shooting had occurred in a parking lot behind the Chippewa Grill, 822 Chippewa Street, on the East Side of town. Twelve-fifty-eight A.M. of October 11, 1996. Ray Casey was the primary witness. Ray Casey would be interviewed many times. Fact is, Ray had been making the rounds of the East Side taverns. Since the break-up with Teena he'd been spending more and more time alone, drinking. Driving his car along the river to Youngstown and back. Stopping at country taverns where no one would have heard of *what-happened-to-Teena* on the Fourth of July in Rocky Point Park.

Teena Maguire, who was Ray Casey's lover. Almost they'd decided to live together, in Casey's house. When Casey's divorce came through.

Now you didn't dare speak to him about Teena Maguire. Not a word about any of it.

Casey had near about cracked his estranged wife across the mouth for certain remarks she'd made about Teena Maguire.

As for Teena she would not see him now. Would not speak with him on the phone. *Ray leave me alone, I'm so tired. I don't want your pity. Somebody better put me out of my mercy. I mean misery.*

He felt so guilty about Teena! Wanted to love her like he'd done but she wasn't the same person now. Never would be again. The hurt was deep inside her, it would never be healed.

Or maybe Casey had not loved her enough. That was the test, maybe. A woman raped by how many men: even she didn't know.

At the Chippewa Grill, Casey had not been in a belligerent mood. This could not be claimed against him by witnesses like the other time, at Mack's Tavern. It was DeLucca who'd sighted Casey and recognized him. Are you following me, asshole? DeLucca had asked. Casey looked blank at him not seeming to know who the hell DeLucca was. But when he left the tavern there was DeLucca waiting to jump him.

Dromoor happened to be at the Chippewa, too. Off-duty. Not in his police officer's uniform and he didn't much resemble a cop wearing a ratty gray sweatshirt, khakis. Dromoor, too, was drinking in a neighborhood several miles from his own. Why this was, Dromoor could not say. He offered no explanation. It just was. He had not shaved for two days and his jaws were covered in stubble like wires. At the bar Dromoor drank three glasses of ale: Black Horse. Watched TV, Roy Jones, Jr. outboxing an opponent in Vegas, bloodying the man's face humiliating him through twelve excruciating rounds without knocking him out like that's too much trouble. Dromoor admired cruel-sly boxers like Jones, all over his opponent and inside his head and makes it look easy like some kind of dance. Dromoor watched TV but refrained from commenting on it like others at the bar one of whom was Ray Casey who was more vociferous, the kind of guy who talks to the TV screen like he's expecting it to talk back.

Was it possible, Dromoor and Casey were aware of each other without so much as glancing at each other like creatures of identical species among natural enemies?

No news reports would suggest this. No official statements issued by the NFPD would suggest this.

Approximately 12:30 A.M., Dromoor decided to leave.

Going where?

Home.

A coincidence, Dromoor decided to leave the tavern

almost immediately after Ray Casey left. Casey whom Dro-moor had not seen at the bar, to whom he certainly had not spoken. Dromoor was leaving a few minutes after Jimmy DeLucca, also undetected, had left, slipping outside to wait for Casey in the parking lot.

Must've been like this. The chronology of events. What links events is never so clear as the events themselves.

Possibly, Casey used the men's room on his way out. Pos-sibly, Dromoor did, too.

Such things aren't planned. Definitely, they are not rehearsed. You get one time, only.

This thing with DeLucca, Casey: possibly there'd been tension in the air, at the bar. Possibly these two had been aware of each other. Guys hating each other's guts. One of them thinking the other has got a serious grudge against him, he'd better take the first strike.

It feels like instinct. Deep in the gut. You'd have to know the men's personal histories to know otherwise.

Casey would insist, he hadn't been drinking heavily. Not for him. Only just beer. Shit, he could handle beer. He had a DWI since the thing with Teena Maguire and for sure did not want a repeat. Still, his judgment was somewhat impaired. Must've been. Why take such a risk, if he'd been fully sober? DeLucca spoke to him, or of him, a certain epi-thet to which Casey took offense. Possibly Casey only over-heard this epithet, but knew it meant him. At another time and in another mood Casey wouldn't have risked fighting with this juiced-up punk a decade younger than he was, and twenty pounds heavier. But Casey was in the mood.

He used the men's room. He left the tavern. Outside in the parking lot the juiced-up punk was waiting.

Just came at me, Casey would say. Marveling, almost.

Just came at me unprovoked. Drunk son of a bitch saying he was gonna kill me.

At this time, approximately 12:55 A.M., Dromoor was exiting the tavern. Immediately he heard the men's raised voices. He understood this was a fight, he would break it up. Dromoor had no hesitation acting on his own, without a fellow officer. His instinct was to move in the direction of any disturbance of the peace, to intercede. Before he saw the struggling men he heard Casey being beaten: groaning, crying out in pain. And another man grunting, and cursing. When Dromoor came closer he saw that Casey was fallen, and DeLucca was kicking him in the groin area. From out of his jacket pocket DeLucca drew a weapon: a switchblade Dromoor estimated to be between six and eight inches in length.

Immediately Dromoor called out identifying himself as a NFPD officer. He instructed the aggressor to throw down his knife, to keep his hands where Dromoor could see them. DeLucca cursed Dromoor and continued to kick at Casey, who was bleeding from the mouth. DeLucca began to make swiping gestures at Casey with the knife, missing the fallen man's face by a fraction of an inch.

Now Dromoor was running. Showing his NFPD shield. DeLucca made a certain obscene gesture at Dromoor with the switchblade and told him to keep the hell away. Dromoor continued to advance, now drawing his weapon. It was clear to DeLucca, both Dromoor and Casey would testify, that

DeLucca saw Dromoor's weapon, and heard his instructions. Dromoor ordered DeLucca to drop the knife. Dromoor ordered DeLucca to step away from Casey. Instead, DeLucca lunged forward, swiping at Dromoor with the knife, and Dromoor fired two shots in the area of the aggressor's heart, from a distance of less than three inches. DeLucca stumbled backward at once, dying.

It was over within seconds. It was nothing like Roy Jones, Jr. tormenting an opponent through twelve long rounds.

Afterward Casey would claim that the police officer had saved his life! Absolutely.

Crazy drunk guy wanting to kill me, saying he was gonna cut my throat like a hog's. I guess he knew who I was. I never knew who he was till after. Then it made sense.

The wildest luck, Dromoor had come along.

And you and Police Officer Dromoor were not acquainted?

No. We were not.

You did not know that Dromoor was a police officer until he identified himself?

I had no awareness of him previously. In the tavern, I had not seen him.

And you did not recognize James DeLucca?

Definitely I did not.

Though James DeLucca was one of the accused in the rape case involving your friend Martine Maguire?

Must've been he looked different than he had. Or I never saw his face too clear.

You would learn DeLucca's identity only after his death? This would be a total surprise to you?

I am totally surprised every day in my life. This was not so astonishing to me.

Dromoor was interrogated at NFPD headquarters.

Dromoor had shot and killed a man in alleged self-defense. There was a civilian witness to corroborate his statement, but only one witness. The shooting was widely reported in area newspapers and on TV. Much was made of the fact that the dead man was scheduled to be tried on charges of rape and aggravated assault along with several others in what was locally called the boathouse rape case.

And you were entirely unaware of the identity of James DeLucca at the time of the incident?

Yes, Detective. I was unaware.

It was a total surprise to you, to learn James DeLucca's identity after the fact?

No, Detective. It was not a total surprise.

It was not, Officer? And why not?

Dromoor remained silent for a long moment, frowning at his clasped hands. His hair, recently cut, gave off a sullen glow, like pewter. The interview was being taped. Dromoor spoke slowly, each word to be chosen with care.

Because I am not surprised by much in life, Detective.

You did not recognize James DeLucca, though you had seen him in a courtroom at close range, hardly a month ago when you'd given a statement in a case involving DeLucca?

I did not see DeLucca's face clearly in the parking lot, I had not seen him in the tavern.

And were you and Raymond Casey acquainted before the shooting?

No, Detective. We were not.

You did not know of Raymond Casey's connection with Martine Maguire at the time of the shooting?

No, Detective. I did not.

It was purely a coincidence, was it? Like a shake of the dice? You, and Raymond Casey, and James DeLucca in a parking lot together, and no other witnesses? Only just what comes up, comes up? Only just chance?

Dromoor knew he was being baited. But would not acknowledge it as if to acknowledge it would be to diminish both his own and his interrogator's dignity.

No, Detective. Not just chance.

Like what then, Officer?

Like it was meant to be. Like if there is God, or even if there is not. There was a purpose, and I discharged my sworn duty as a police officer.

Dromoor was not penalized beyond thirty days' desk assignment. He surrendered his police service revolver for thirty days. It would be thirty days before he returned to active duty, and by this time he would be in training as a detective at the Eighth Precinct. The older detectives liked Dromoor, he listened respectfully and intelligently and rarely spoke unless spoken to. When they interrogated suspects and when they discussed cases Dromoor observed them with the attentiveness of a young raptor among his elders. Soon he was accompanying the Eighth Precinct's senior detective, helping to secure crime scenes, taking photographs. It was a good time for Dromoor. He felt good about the future. *Eye for an eye, tooth for a tooth.* In time.

Double-Edged Knife

IN TIME YOU WOULD fall in love with other men. More appropriate men. Men your own age, or nearly. You would marry a man older than you by eleven years, when you were twenty-one. But you would never love any of these men the way in your desperation and yearning you had loved John Dromoor in your adolescence.

Not until years afterward would you realize *I loved him for Momma's sake, too. Because she could not.*

So it had been a double love. Dangerously sharp, like a double-edged knife.

Vanished!

MARVIN PICK, LLOYD PICK. One day in late October 1996, the two prime defendants in the Rocky Point rape case simply vanished.

One day word was out in Niagara County Courthouse circles that their lawyer, Jay Kirkpatrick, was negotiating a remarkable plea bargain with prosecutors for his clients in which charges of rape were to be dropped and "aggravated assault" would be lowered to the much lesser "assault"—and the next day the brothers had vanished.

It was assumed the Picks had jumped bail. They would not be seen again in Niagara Falls. Their family and relatives would not hear from them. After their initial arrest in the rape case the brothers had spoken recklessly of crossing the border into Canada, not at Niagara Falls but at some low-security crossing like Youngstown or Fort Niagara, make their way to the west or better yet the Northwest Territory where it was said able-bodied young guys like them could find jobs in lumbering, fishery canning, salmon fishing. And good wages, too.

Since before the trouble Marv had been laid off from

Niagara Natural Gas for eight months anyway. Lloyd was having trouble keeping a job and these were shithead jobs anyway: busboy at Luigo's Pizzeria, lawn crew for County Parks and Recreation. In the Northwest Territory of Canada it was said to be raw frontier like one hundred years ago in the northwestern United States. Employers did not scrutinize employees closely. Nobody gave a damn about education, past record, background. If the brothers weren't Canadian citizens, hell, they could be "issued work visas," Marv had heard.

Marvin Pick, Lloyd Pick. After the arrests the brothers carried themselves with a certain public swagger. In their neighborhood it wasn't said of the Picks they'd raped, almost killed a woman and terrorized the woman's daughter, it was said *Those two! Their old man has hired a hot-shit Buffalo lawyer.*

The father Walt Pick was fifty-seven years old. A veteran welder at Tyler Pipe. A heavy-set coarser-skinned replica of the sons lacking their tufted sand-colored hair. His eyes were recessed in the ridges of his face with the slow-smoldering look of a welding iron. Where Marv and Lloyd had lifted weights, body-built their torsos into armor and their necks thick as hams, Walt Pick was naturally big, beefy. He stood only five feet nine but weighed two hundred forty pounds. When informed that his out-on-bail sons had disappeared, left Marv's car behind at Fort Niagara State Park, Walt had had to sit down, he'd been so shocked.

"Those fuckers! Sons of bitches! Jumping bail! All I done

for them! All I done for them!" Hot tears sprang into Walt's eyes. He was not a man susceptible to emotions of much subtlety. In the course of a day he swerved between irascibility and phlegmatic affability. He could be good-natured. He was given to say that he lived for summers, his outboard boat. Fishing on Lake Ontario off his brother's place at Olcott. He was a family man, too. He'd been married to Irma for thirty-three years. Six kids, most of them okay. The girls were the ones he'd most worried over. Marv and Lloyd, they'd always been trouble. Marv especially. And now this.

For each of the Pick brothers, as for the other defendants in the case, bail had been set at $75,000. The actual sum paid out by Walt Pick, to a bail bondsman, had been $7,500 each. It was the goddamned lawyer whose fee was astronomical: Kirkpatrick demanded a retainer of $30,000 for each brother. His hourly fee was $250 out of court, $350 in court. There would be other fees, Walt Pick didn't doubt. The Pick family, like the families of the other defendants, had had to take out a second mortgage on their home. Walt Pick had been humbled, forced to borrow from relatives. He'd had to sell, at a heartbreaking loss, his twenty-foot motorboat on whose scummy white prow was hand-painted in red letters *Condor II*.

Irma Pick believed fiercely that her sons were innocent, but Walt guessed they were guilty as hell. They'd been in trouble with the law before. And some of it female trouble. The other girls had not dared to press charges with the police but the others had not been hurt as badly as the Maguire woman. Walt was informed this was serious, rape and aggravated assault were serious felonies, his sons could be sent to Attica for thirty years. Thirty years! They'd be old men when they got out. Old as their old man now. If they got out at all.

Walt was advised by Father Muldoon, the pastor of St. Timothy's Parish: hire the best damn criminal lawyer you can afford, he will plea-bargain the charges down to less than ten years, and for Lloyd, being younger, maybe less. If the boys behaved themselves in prison they could be out in as few as four or five years.

Jay Kirkpatrick was the man. Kirkpatrick will cost you an arm and a leg and your left testicle but Kirkpatrick is the man.

Others had spoken of Kirkpatrick, too. The Haabers had the idea the defendants should hire a "legal team." Like O. J. Simpson, that kind of strategy. They could pool their resources. Kirkpatrick would be Marv's and Lloyd's lawyer but provide advice to the other lawyers. A team of lawyers, not individuals. A team made you think of sports, a game. A good rough game, that if you had Kirkpatrick as head coach, you might win.

Walt said shit, far as he was concerned it was no-win. It was lose-lose. His hard-earned money and *Condor II* down the drain. Goddamn those sons of his!

He'd hired Kirkpatrick, though. Like a gambler risking all his cash on a toss of the dice.

You had to be impressed with Kirkpatrick. An hour's interview with the boys and already he'd allowed them and their father to see how "rape" could be reinterpreted as "consensual sex"—"sex-for-hire." The Maguire woman had been drinking, her testimony was shaky. A good cross-examination and she'd be discredited. And the daughter allegedly hiding in a corner of the boathouse had not actually seen anyone rape anyone by her own account. She could not testify that other young men had not entered the boathouse and raped her mother after the departure of the Picks and their companions.

Kirkpatrick said, "There are two sides to every story, in a trial. The winning side, and the other."

Walt whistled through his teeth. Here was genius!

Even so, Walt tried to reason with Jay Kirkpatrick. It was unfair, Walt argued, that, because he had two sons on trial, he had to pay double. For two clients charged with exactly the same crimes would not require nearly so much legal effort as two separate clients charged with two separate crimes, would they? How could they?

"It's like twins, right? A woman has two babies, they ain't actually twice as much work as two would be, another time. Everybody knows that. That's why a woman has two breasts. Ask any woman."

Walt had hoped for a discount of maybe 10 percent. Kirkpatrick smiled and said Walt would make a damn good lawyer, arguing so precisely. Except a discount was not possible.

"I am an attorney, Mr. Pick. I am not a remnant carpet store."

Marvin Pick, Lloyd Pick. They'd been high school wrestlers. On the East Side Marv was admired if not much liked. Lloyd was his lieutenant. Always he'd been the emotional brother, hobbled by the rudiments of conscience like a horse with a pebble in its hoof. Now he was blaming Marv for the trouble he'd gotten them into.

"Fuck you, asshole. You were the one said, 'Let's jump those two cunts.'"

"I did not! Fuck I never said that! Marv, *I did not.*"

Lloyd was excitable these days, tears springing into his eyes. Marv just laughed. Now that Jay Kirkpatrick was their *legal counsel* he was feeling almost laid back. "Don't worry, Lloyd. I ain't going to in-form. I ain't going to turn state's witness." Since the intrusion of the Niagara County criminal justice machine into the Picks' lives, Marv's vocabulary had expanded.

Marvin Pick, Lloyd Pick. Before the boathouse incident they'd been picked up for local break-ins, lifting merchandise at Home Depot and Kmart, an attempted carjacking. They'd been arrested, pleaded guilty on the advice of their legal defense lawyer, served minimal juvie time. Marv saw that the criminal justice system was crowded with black guys, some of them really scary gangsta types, stone-cold killers at fifteen, him and Lloyd didn't look so threatening, somehow.

Their cousin Nate Baumdollar, whose father, part owner of a tavern and bowling alley in Lackawanna, was believed to be "mobbed up," told the brothers they were assholes, the bunch of them, not to finish the job and dump the females in the lagoon. Both of them. "See, now you wouldn't be up shit crick. 'Eyewitnesses.' Bet you never thought of it, none of you, huh? Shit-for-brains." Nate brayed with laughter. He was Marv's age. All their lives the two had been hateful of each other but thrown together to "play" at family outings.

Marv protested, "We wasn't gonna kill her, come on. It was never anything like that. Only just, we got out of there and left her. Joe said she was bleeding like a damn pig, if nobody found her and called the cops that was it."

"Dumping her," Lloyd said, nerved up, picking at his nose, "would be something you could prove. For sure, they'd get you then."

"Get who, asshole? *I* wasn't there."

Marv said with sudden vehemence, "That's right, fuck-face. You weren't there. So shut up."

Nate laughed. He liked it that Walt Pick had approached his old man for a loan, having to humble himself to his brother-in-law, and Nate's shrewd old man had said sure, Walt, but there's 12 percent interest. And we get the document notarized.

Marv said, aggrieved, "She asked for it. Fucking Teena. I seen her around, I know her. She knows me, too! She was showing her ass and her damn boobs. She was plenty hot. She said, 'What you guys got in your pants? Are you hot, or what?' "

Lloyd looked at him, incredulous. This was all fanciful stuff, like what came out of Kirkpatrick's mouth was contagious.

Marv continued, inspired, addressing Nate like Nate was the Jew judge Schpiro, "She said she'd suck us off for ten bucks each. If there was ten of us, we'd get a discount: nine bucks each. She did! You can laugh but she did! She's a hooker junkie. Anybody in the neighborhood will tell you. Some people, they came to Father Muldoon to tell him what they knew about Teena Maguire, if it was needed to be known for our sake. Our attorney Mr. Kirkpatrick he's gonna get witnesses from like her high school, guys who knew her way back, establish a pattern of 'promiscuous and reckless sexual behavior' to present to the jury. He's already got witnesses testifying she was falling-down drunk and high on coke before we ever saw her. Before she ever got to the fucking park. And the daughter, see it was some kind of mother-daughter deal. Like, two-for-one. The little cunt was half price."

Lloyd said, squirming with sudden excitement, "That girl! She saw my face, I guess. Must've picked out my picture. And in the damn lineup she collared me. And there's bloodstains, and other stuff. Wish to hell I'd known what was coming, this girl, this kid, putting the finger on me." He shook his head, mute in anguish.

Nate crowed, "See? You assholes? What I told you, I'd of been there, you needed to finish the job and dump 'em both. Tied down with rocks. Save your old man having to sell his boat."

Marv Pick, Lloyd Pick. Marv had a dagger/flaming heart tattoo on his left forearm, Lloyd had a greasy black coiled cobra on his. When they'd wrestled as kids, thumping and thudding on the floor of their room or downstairs in the living room, Irma screamed at them the entire house was shaking. Of course Marv, always heavier than Lloyd by ten–fifteen pounds, and meaner, always won.

The night before the brothers vanished, leaving Marv's 1989 bronze Taurus in a parking lot at Fort Niagara State Park, they were observed driving in this vehicle slow along Baltic Avenue. Slow to the corner of Baltic and Chautauqua. Slow past the Kevecki house at 2861 Baltic. They were drinking beer. Hell, they'd put away most of a case of Coors, fast. They were excited but also aggrieved. They were in a brooding mood but also edgy. They were not exactly sorry for what they'd done because they could not clearly recall any single moment in which they had made a conscious decision to "do" anything to anyone whether sexual, violent, rough-play, or whatever, and so they did not consider themselves responsible, somehow. Their dad was the one taking this hardest. *He* was sure looking sorry. Their mom was an excitable loyal mom who refused to believe any of this could be serious, that felony crap the prosecutors were threatening. *Her word against theirs* their mom said. *And that woman a drunk and a whore.* Their mom wasn't wanting to think about how much this was costing. Maybe couldn't face thinking about it like: What if they lost their house? Where'd they live? That cocksucker Nate was right: their dad's boat. Christ, Marv and Lloyd loved that boat, too! It was fucking boring out there on fucking Lake Ontario where it was always windy and clouding up to rain fishing with the old man but made you sick at heart to think *Condor II* was gone, you would not ever go fishing with Dad again. Not ever.

Kirkpatrick who was their *legal counsel* had instructed

them: no talking about the case, and no approaching the Maguire woman and her daughter.

How many times they'd been told, the gang of them: stay away from Baltic Avenue.

No cruising west of the park to intimidate the Maguires or any other witnesses who'd seen them in the park that night. (There were a lot of these witnesses. Fucking cops had really tossed out a net.) No trying to contact the Maguires. Not Martine, not the daughter, and not the grandmother. Or any other relative. The judge had okayed something called an injunction. Meaning stay away.

Certain of the cops in the Eighth Precinct who'd roughed them up that night bringing them in, had been more explicit. Warning the guys they'd bust their balls if they were caught even west of the park, in the Maguires' neighborhood.

Marv and Lloyd weren't thinking of that now. They'd become kind of buddies now. Bonded it was called. Like soldiers. At war. This was a war, like. These people trying to destroy them. Not just them, their parents. And Jimmy DeLucca, he'd been shot down dead the other night by a NFPD cop off-duty! So there's cops on the street you can't identify. Cops with concealed weapons. Mostly Marv and Lloyd were pissed at DeLucca lately so they weren't wasting many tears on him, it was the principle of the thing. DeLucca was the one said *We could toss a firebomb into the old lady's house, show the cunt she better back off* and Marv had told DeLucca he was an asshole everybody'd know who did it, they'd be back in Niagara Men's Detention and their bail revoked. Like Joe Rickert, parole revoked and he's back in Olean sweating his ass he won't get transferred to Attica.

Somehow, the good Coors buzz and resentment commingled and there was Marv leaning out his rolled-down window as for the third or maybe fourth time the Taurus cruised past the frumpy-looking red-brick house at 2861 Baltic Avenue where the windows were lighted downstairs and blinds drawn tight and Marv was bawling, "Teeeeena!" and when Lloyd poked him in the ribs he laughed, gunned the motor, and burned rubber making his escape.

Marv Pick, Lloyd Pick. The call came for Marv. Late afternoon of October 27. There was this man's voice, unfamiliar. And the name he identified himself by, that Marv didn't catch. The caller spoke with an air of authority that put Marv in mind of Mr. Kirkpatrick and so it was no surprise that the caller explained he was a "legal investigator" for Jay Kirkpatrick and that he had some "photographic evidence" for Marvin Pick and Lloyd Pick that had to be delivered to them as Mr. Kirkpatrick's clients by a third party, an intermediary. There were complicated legal reasons requiring secrecy. Mr. Kirkpatrick could not be actively involved. "As a lawyer, he is an 'officer of the court.' He is required to turn over to the court any and all evidence pertaining to a crime that comes into his hands. These photographs, which incriminate the witnesses against you, will come to you from another party." Marv tried to follow this. It sounded urgent. He gestured for Lloyd to be quiet.

Marv was dry-mouthed listening to instructions. Evidence! Incriminate witnesses! Mr. Kirkpatrick's legal investigator was telling him that he and his brother Lloyd would have to leave the city for the transfer of materials. For legal reasons, the transaction could not take place inside the city limits of Niagara Falls. They were to drive to Fort Niagara State Park off Route 18. They were to exit west into the park, and a quarter mile inside the park on the right there's a turnoff where the caller would be waiting in his vehicle, which would be parked facing him, roll down his window, and the caller would hand over the Wendy's box and both vehicles would then be driven away. No conversation. No witnesses.

Marv pleaded with the caller would he please repeat the instructions. Christ! He didn't want to make any mistake.

Marv Pick, Lloyd Pick. Told their mom who was always anxious now where they were going and who with like they were grade school kids not adults in their twenties not to wait supper for them they'd be out for a while. In Marv's car north on Route 18 to Fort Niagara at the windy-roughened edge of Lake Ontario, where the Niagara River rushes into the lake. Just across the bridge is Ontario, Canada. In summer the park was swarming with people, in late October, on a cold day, sky above the lake riddled with bruises and pitholes like rotted spots in fruit, and a mean wind rolling off the water, the place was deserted.

Marv said, " 'Legal investigator.' That's some guy like a private detective, he's on your side. Not the cops'. "

Marv followed the caller's precise directions. It was nearing dusk when they entered Fort Niagara State Park. It's always a shock to see the lake, the water so close. Where the river rushed into the lake the hard blue water moved in long shudders.

"Think that's him? The 'legal investigator'?"

A station wagon parked up ahead. Facing the entrance. Lloyd only grunted knowing his brother wasn't asking an actual question.

With restrained eagerness Marv drove the Taurus bumping along the rutted and rain-puddled roadway. He pulled up beside the station wagon, a Ford, not new, that had hanging from its inside rearview mirror a pair of tiny white baby's shoes. If he'd had time to think the baby shoes would have placated him. *A legal investigator, working for Mr. Kirkpatrick. But just a family guy, like anybody.*

The driver was wearing a Buffalo Bills cap pulled low over his forehead. He appeared to have no hair, the sides of his head were shaved bullet-smooth. Though it was past sunset he was wearing dark glasses. Marv braked his car, rolled down the window smiling in nervous anticipation.

"I guess you got something for us? Me an' Lloyd?"

In the late morning of the following day the bronze Taurus, left not in a parking place but in the middle of the puddled roadway, would be examined by a New York State trooper called to the scene by park authorities. The car was unlocked, the key was in the ignition. The gas gauge showed a quarter-full tank. There appeared to be no recent damage to the car. A case of Coors in the backseat, three cans remaining. The trooper called in the license plate and learned that the car was registered to one Marvin Pick, Eleventh Street, Niagara Falls. Pick was registered as out on bail awaiting trial in Niagara Falls for several felonies.

Eventually, the Taurus was towed from the park and impounded as evidence. Rumor on the street and in the NFPD Eighth Precinct was, the Picks had jumped bail and fled into Canada. Their bail would be retained by the county. Their father Walt Pick would declare bankruptcy and die of a stroke within eighteen months. Within a few hours of the discovery of the Taurus, Marvin Pick and Lloyd Pick would be reclassified as *fugitives from justice, should be considered dangerous*.

"Teeeeena!"

Y OU WERE VERY FRIGHTENED. Standing at the upstairs window the room in darkness behind you. Watching as the bronze car on oversized tires cruised taunting-slow past the house.

Turning right onto the next street. Circling the block, returning to cruise past the house the driver leaning out the window showing his face.

You thought *It's them. Come back to finish the job.*

You wondered if your mother heard. She was locked away in her old, girlhood room at the rear of the house.

Momma had not eaten dinner. You had not seen her for two days. *Sober* was not much cherished by Teena Maguire. *Sober* is no protection against your thoughts.

"Hey Teeeeena! Teeeeena!"

They'd circled the block another time. Marvin Pick, you recognized. Just one other guy with him, must be his brother Lloyd.

You wondered if in their sick way they loved Teena Maguire. They loved how they'd broken her, made her their own. In the courtroom you had entered trustingly, when the rapists' lawyer had uttered his terrible words like curses, you'd seen how avidly the rapists had watched your mother. The Pick brothers with their smoldering recessed eyes and part-opened mouths.

"Teeeeena!"

Hyena laughter. Tires screeching in a quick getaway.

Except: you'd seen. You were the witness, clearly you had seen.

You'd given Dromoor's cell phone number to your mother as he'd asked you. But of course you'd memorized it first.

Help us please help us John Dromoor we are so afraid.

Hawk

K_{EEEEER–R–R}!

The hawk's cry, startled-sounding and shrill. Mixed with the wind like it was, you weren't sure what you were hearing.

Soon after the call from Teena's daughter, Dromoor drove out to Fort Niagara State Park. Wanting to check out the site.

He was off-duty, in civilian clothes. Still, Dromoor carried his weapon.

A cop is never off-duty. A cop is always a cop.

Let his mind drift and settle. See what's here. Rocky shore, slate-blue mean-looking water in ceaseless waves crashing against pebbly sand. He was watching hawks rising out of pines along the bluff, rising to maybe hundreds of feet, in their hunt.

Predator birds these were. Fascinating.

Dromoor did not know the names of these dark-feathered broad-tailed birds other than *hawk*.

Some species of hawk that, as they rose into the air, from beneath you could see a flash of white on the underside of the tail. And that weird squealing cry: *Keeeeer-r-r!*

Reminded him of Teena. *Teeeeena.*

It was notable how, high overhead, the hawks became suddenly weightless. They scarcely needed to move their wings. The wind bore them as if they were swimming. The wind was the hawks' element as completely as if these gusts, random in velocity and in direction, were but the hawks' breaths.

He squinted watching one of the hawks. How, beginning its downward plunge, it accelerated its speed. Jesus! Took your breath away how the bird swooped, seized its prey in beak and wings, and bore it aloft again in a single fluid motion.

Dromoor owned a rifle, now. He was coming to see the beauty of a sleek long-barreled gun, smooth-gleaming wood stock. Yet he would not wish to shoot one of these birds. He would not wish to shoot any living creature except in self-defense or in defense of another.

Help us please help us John Dromoor we are so afraid.

He felt good about DeLucca. He believed in justice but not in the judicial instruments of justice. *Eye for an eye, tooth for a tooth.*

Taking the law into your own hands, fuck what's wrong with that?

Dromoor smiled. Thinking he trusted his own damn hands, not anybody else's.

Letting his mind soar and drift. Scarcely needing to think, he would trust his instinct. He was still soaring with the high from shooting the rapist DeLucca, many times he'd replayed the squeezing of his trigger finger, instanteous *crack!* and the target immediately collapsing, falling to the ground.

Casey had been awed. Casey had not known what to expect but Jesus there it was.

Once you squeeze the trigger if you knew what you were doing your target is gone.

Once your target is gone, he doesn't testify against you.

NFPD Internal Affairs had ruled self-defense in the DeLucca shooting. There had never been much doubt inside the precinct but still IA might have ruled excessive force, which would mean an indictment for Police Officer Dromoor on a count of first-degree manslaughter.

A more serious charge, second-degree homicide, had never been likely.

At the precinct the verdict had been met with much approval, enthusiasm. The media, ever vigilant in the Maguire rape case, seemed to concur. When Officer Dromoor was approached for comment he would say tersely "No comment." Dromoor was perceived as a somber, frowning man. Husband, father of small children. Not one to be inveigled by the media into saying anything questionable nor even allowing himself to be photographed looking other than somber, frowning.

Self-defense is the best offense Officer Dromoor believed. Not likely he'd tell the media this.

And now he was training to be a detective. His mind seemed to work pretty well that way, too. A police officer on the street is quick reflexes and a sharp eye for danger, a detective is more like playing chess. It's a game and you have time to make your move. You can see the other guy's moves, right out there on the board. What you can't see, you have to

figure out. What's a detective but a guy using his brains figuring out, If I did this crime, why'd I do it? And who am I?
Dromoor liked that feeling.

It was seeing around two corners not just one. Sometimes, three.

Like, not calling Teena Maguire from any phone to be
traced to Dromoor. Not ever. If Teena chose to call Officer
Dromoor, that could be explained.

Like, firing two shots into DeLucca's heart. As Dromoor
had been trained.

In the U.S. Army as at Police Academy shooting instruc-
tors repeated: You don't owe the enemy the first shot.

Some people, the instinct is strong not to kill. Not to
hurt. Their instinct is dangerous to their survival, and has to
be overcome.

Dromoor had not been born with that instinct, apparently. If he had, it had died in the Persian desert. His inchworm soul coiling up and dying in the hot sun.

His wife accused him, sometimes. Not she didn't love
him like crazy but she was scared of him, a little. Saying she
never knew where his mind was and what he was thinking
even when they were making love sometimes she knew *It's
some other woman is it?* Dromoor only just laughed, wouldn't
dignify such a question by any reply.

He had a way of not answering that had become more
pronounced in the past few years. His wife believed it had to
do with him becoming a cop, carrying a gun. Seeing the
kind of ugly things a street cop sees.

In fact Dromoor wasn't in love with Teena Maguire.

He didn't think so. It wasn't that. Not so simple.

Just some feeling he had about her, and the girl. The daughter.

Because he'd been the first on the scene. Maybe that was why. He was the one.

Now he walked along the bluff above the lake for approximately thirty minutes. Met no one, you wouldn't expect to. It was damn cold out here. Returned to his station wagon, smiling to see Robbie's baby shoes hanging from the mirror. He guessed, the Picks saw those baby shoes, they'd have a good feeling.

Watching the hawks, he'd made his decision. Not even thinking but just watching the hawks.

Dromoor felt good about DeLucca. He seemed to know, he'd feel even better about the Picks.

How Things Work Out

CASEY WAS GONE AT last from Teena Maguire's life. He had ceased telephoning, for his calls were not returned. He would not again humble himself coming to the house on Baltic Avenue as, one Friday evening in November, he'd driven over uninvited and was told by Teena's embarrassed mother Agnes Kevecki that Teena was not home.

Saying, "Teena has gone out, Ray. I'm not sure where."

Casey had been drinking, you could see. But he was clean-shaven and somber in appearance. He had always liked Teena's mother, and she had liked him though she had not approved of Teena "seeing" a married man with young children.

"Who with, Agnes? D'you know who with?"

Casey's voice broke, enunciating *who with*.

"Ray, I'm afraid I do not."

Casey nodded. All right. He must see the logic of this, probably he knew it was for the best.

"Tell Teena I love her, okay? Can't say I'm gonna miss her because I been missing her since, you know. Since that night. So tell her good-bye, will you?"

"Yes, Ray. I will."

You'd been upstairs on the stairway landing, listening. You knew maybe you should come downstairs, say good-bye to Casey, too. But you held back. Just didn't want to see him. Didn't want to risk crying.

Soon after you would hear that Ray Casey was "reunited" with his family. There was talk of Casey and his wife selling their house, moving over to Grand Island, maybe Tonawanda. Out of Niagara Falls where there's too many bad memories.

For the best Teena said. *Maybe it is God's will. How things work out.*

Media Frenzy

LOCAL TELEVISION, RADIO NEWS. Newspapers. Tabloids. Since the headlining on the morning of July 5, 1996, of the sensational ROCKY POINT GANG RAPE it was rare for more than a few days to pass in Niagara Falls and vicinity without ROCKY POINT RAPE CASE figuring prominently in local news. GANG RAPE: MOTHER, DAUGHTER VICTIMS? was a far more intriguing headline than the usual headlines concerning contaminated land-fills, EPA lawsuits against local chemical factories and oil refineries. Through July/August/September/October you could not escape the inch-high headlines and their accompanying photographs, often in full color.

NOTED BUFFALO ATTORNEY KIRKPATRICK ENGAGED
IN DEFENSE OF FALLS YOUTHS ACCUSED
OF GANG RAPE

NIAGARA CO. GRAND JURY INDICTS 8 FALLS YOUTHS
July 4th Gang-Rape, Rocky Point Park

RAPE: A LOVE STORY

SCHPIRO NAMED ROCKY POINT RAPE TRIAL JUDGE

DEFENDANTS PLEAD "NOT GUILTY" IN ROCKY POINT RAPE TRIAL

The tabloids were not so restrained. You would see some of these by chance, on newsstands or in stores. You would wish to quickly avert your eyes but sometimes could not. TEENA blazoned on the front pages of these publications signaled TEENA MAGUIRE, ALLEGED GANG-RAPE VICTIM whose story was many times recycled, with variants, on inside pages. The tabloids had offered your mother thousands of dollars in return for her "confidential" story but your mother had not replied. You too had been approached, and had literally run away. (Reporters and photographers waited for you outside Baltic Junior High, the first week of school.) Soon then the tabloids turned nasty: TEENA CHALLENGED BY ALLEGED RAPISTS: SEX CONSENSUAL, FOR $?

The most sensational of the local tabloids ran lengthy interviews with mothers of the several of the "alleged rapists," including Mrs. Pick, Mrs. DeLucca, and Mrs. Haaber. One of these, ripped from the paper and shoved inside your locker at school, was headlined GRIEVING MOTHER VOWS "DEFAMATION" LAWSUIT AGAINST TEENA: *"That Woman Has Destroyed My Son's Life."*

Eventually, there were unexpected developments. Even larger headlines, photographs.

DELUCCA, 24, SHOT AND KILLED BY
NFPD OFF-DUTY OFFICER
DEFENDANT IN ROCKY POINT GANG-RAPE CASE

DELUCCA SHOOTING BY OFF-DUTY NFPD OFFICER
DROMOOR
RULED SELF-DEFENSE AFTER INVESTIGATION

And in late October:

PICK BROTHERS VANISH FROM FT. NIAGARA PARK
Defendants in Rocky Point Rape Case Missing

PICK BROTHERS "JUMP BAIL" SAY POLICE
DECLARED FUGITIVES

FALLS BROTHERS JOIN "MOST WANTED" LIST

After a press conference hurriedly called by Jay Kirkpatrick:

HIS CLIENTS "HOUNDED" OUT OF U.S. BY POLICE
DEFENSE LAWYER KIRKPATRICK CLAIMS

And:

ONTARIO PROVINCIAL POLICE REPORT "NO SIGHTINGS"
OF MISSING DEFENDANTS IN ROCKY POINT RAPE CASE
Nationwide Alert, Royal Canadian Mounted Police

Grandma was always saying, "Hide these damn things from Teena, Bethie. She doesn't need to be reminded."

Yet Teena must have known. Since DeLucca's death, and since the Pick brothers had vanished, you could see that your mother was less anxious. *She and Dromoor keep in touch. That must be.*

You felt a stab of jealousy, you knew so little about Dromoor.

The Picks had been the ones who'd frightened Teena most. She had believed there was no escape from Marvin Pick in particular. He had been the one to accost her, initially. He had known her, and she had known him, if only slightly. Screaming *Teeeeena!* and grabbing at her and the others roused to frenzy, in his wake.

Even if the Picks had been convicted and sent to prison, one day they would be eligible for parole. They would return to Niagara Falls bent on revenge. Teena had this fixed in her mind, unshakable.

Yet she'd been mistaken, hadn't she? For both Marvin Pick and Lloyd Pick seemed to have vanished. And Teena did not seem to worry that they might be hiding anywhere, and might swoop on her to harm her.

Somehow Teena seemed to know that whether living (in Canada?) or dead (in the choppy waters off Fort Niagara?) neither of the Picks would ever harm her again.

You Lived!

Y OU LIVED THROUGH IT. For years you would live through it and only when you graduated from Baltic Senior High and the cobwebby cohesiveness of *peers, classmates* dissolved with no more resistance than actual cobwebs would you escape it.

There wasn't money for a private school. If you'd transferred to Holy Redeemer, where there were boy and girl cousins of yours, things would have been easier.

But you lived through it. That fall, eighth grade at Baltic Junior High. Approaching the school and in the crowded corridors of the school feeling the eyes move upon you. Those classmates who were related to the rapists or who were their neighbors or friends. Those classmates who were sympathetic with the rapists, the guys, because they'd heard nasty things about Martine Maguire, and about you.

What you were doing was *ratting. Ratting* to the cops, *ratting* to the DA. Nobody likes a *rat*.

You were fearful to enter a lavatory. Girls inside, older girls the meanest. *Her! There she is, damn liar.* In each of the toilet stalls in the girls' lavatory nearest your homeroom, there were lipstick scrawls *HATE B.M.—FUCK BETH M.—* from which you learned to avert your eyes quickly.

On the outside of your locker, through most of eighth grade, you would discover ugly words, drawings in spray paint. School custodians could not remove these easily. Sometimes they didn't remove them for days. B.M. SUKS COKS. FUK B.M. There were clumsy cartoon drawings intended to symbolize, you guessed, female sex organs? You tried to lessen the dramatic impact of these by scratching at them with your fingernails until they became meaningless or even benign symbols, like lopsided suns or moons.

The girls who had lockers on either side of yours pretended not to see. Not the graffiti, and not you.

If

In his eyes you saw it. A tawny yellow gleam as in a video game.

If he hadn't been high on crystal meth. If he hadn't been drunk. If he hadn't been an asshole. Would've been so easy.

Seeing Fritz Haaber, seeing you. On the street. At the mall. Staring at you, face tight as if his skin had shrunk, his teeth and jaws were more prominent, bony bumps in his forehead. Haaber had shaved off his mustache for court appearances. He looked younger, thinner. His hair too had been neatly trimmed. Since Marvin and Lloyd Pick appeared to be out of the trial, the Haabers had borrowed money to hire Kirkpatrick as their lawyer. Except for Fritz Haaber, the remaining defendants had changed their pleas to "guilty" and would negotiate deals with the prosecutors, but Haaber, with his previous assault record, was pleading "not guilty."

So there would be a trial.

Marvin Pick had scared Teena the most, Fritz Haaber scared you.

At the Niagara Mall with your grandmother, you were coming out of JCPenney and there was Haaber walking with another guy. Both wearing reversed baseball caps, sheepskin jackets, soiled jeans. Haaber's yellow eyes moving on you, his face tightening with anger.

Haaber was forbidden to approach you. Haaber was forbidden to speak with you. Yet it was unmistakable, the message he sent.

Oh Christ wishing he'd killed you! Slammed your head against the boathouse floor when he'd had his fucking chance. Broken you with his fists, his stomping feet.

And fucked you, too. When he'd had his chance.

If. If only. Would've been so easy, when he'd had his chance.

So scared, trembling so, Grandma had to drive you home.

You hadn't wanted to tell her about Haaber. She had not seen him, would probably not have known him. There was not much of your life as a thirteen-year-old you told your grandmother about, and even less did you tell your mother.

The stuff at school, all that you spared them. Your worry that Momma would be arrested, charged with contempt of court, if there was a trial and she refused to testify.

Your worry that Momma would die.

You spared the adults in your household. You learned how if a thing is not spoken of, even those closest to you, who love you, will assume that it doesn't exist.

In your marriage, you would cultivate this wisdom.

But you were terrified of Haaber. You seemed to know *He will kill me.* And so you told your grandmother about

him, crying hysterically in the front seat of your grandmother's car. You told your grandmother thinking *She will tell
Momma, Momma will call Dromoor.*

Forgiv Me?

NIGHT OF NOVEMBER 22 three days before the trial was scheduled to begin doused himself with gasoline. Lit a match.

Left behind a note shakily written that would be identified as his handwriting:

God forgiv me and my family I am very ashamed. This will make things right
F. H.

He'd been drinking heavily. He was desperate, he had the shits and red ants were crawling over his brain night and day. At the same time he was goddamned fucking innocent of doing anything to those females and everybody knew this including the females yet he was convinced the jury would not believe him, his lawyer said if he took the witness stand, which it was crucial that Fritz Haaber do, to present his side of things, like how his semen got inside the Maguire female and how her blood got splattered onto his clothes and caked up in the soles of his jogging shoes, the cunt prosecutor could ask about his "past history of abuse toward women," so he was fucked, he was fucked either way, what he'd begun to talk of obsessively was cutting out across the bridge to Canada like those motherfucker Picks, leaving him and the other guys behind, cocksucker traitors, if you want to know the truth it was Marv's idea to gang up on the females, if you want to trace the truth to its source Marv was to blame but Marv was gone, him and Lloyd were gone, and Jimmy DeLucca went nuts and got himself shot down dead like everybody is saying Jimmy must've provoked the cop on purpose, suicide-by-cop it was a known thing, he'd read about in the tabloids and saw on TV. High on crystal meth DeLucca wouldn't know his ass from a hole in the ground, pulling a blade on a guy with a gun. Jesus!

Why hadn't Marv and Lloyd took him with them?! He'd always gotten along with those guys, he thought.

Now it was too late. Customs & Immigration over in Ontario were primed to look for him. All the border crossings between New York and Canada. He'd be arrested and sent back to Niagara Falls in shackles. It was fucking unfair Marv and Lloyd abandoning their friends to clean up their shit after them.

He ever saw them again he'd murder them. Bastards!

Got to make a good impression on the court Kirkpatrick was saying. All the Haabers and any other relatives around should attend every session. Dressed neatly, and sitting where the jurors can see them. Jurors take note of families. Jurors are not very bright but they have certain expectations. Like they would expect Fritz to testify, seeing that he was claiming innocence. They would wish to study his face. Kirkpatrick

believed that jurors in such a case were inclined to sympa-
thize with the defendant if you provided reasonable evidence
for such sympathy. But Fritz's mind drifted when Kirkpatrick
talked. Fucker charging such a "fee" you could not comprehend it. Three hundred fifty per hour in court! And a ball-
buster "retainer." The Haabers were fucked, this was costing
the grandparents, too. Like a taxi meter ticking, a lawyer-
mouth. Once he got this shit behind him if he wasn't sent to
Attica Fritz had got to thinking maybe he'd try to be a
lawyer himself, these guys really made money for just
shooting off their mouths it was mind-fucking. There was
nothing actual to it, being a lawyer. He, Fritz, had worked at
every kind of shit job from Parks & Recreation he'd started
summers in high school to busboy at the Niagara Grand to
driving short-haul lumber and gravel deliveries in secret, he
wasn't a Teamster and could get his head broke if any union
guys caught him. Every kind of degrading shit job you could
imagine but all of them real, actual. None of them just
words. This legal bullshit the lawyers and judge tossed at one
another with straight faces showing this was serious stuff, not
bullshit like everybody including them knew.

This other time he'd been arrested, one of the other
times, previous "assault and battery" when Donna'd had to
go to the ER, she'd testified against him and gotten an
injunction and it was in Fritz' favor she'd been his girlfriend
not some crazy female not of his acquaintance. The judge
had said two years, Fritz had almost shit his pants before the
old fart added to be served on probation, Fritz and his
mother had both been practically bawling, so grateful. But

this time it was different. Kirkpatrick warned him. Not to expect probation if the jury came in with guilty, the judge would give him the maximum. If the jury came in with guilty.

A jury is as bright as the dumbest member of the jury Kirkpatrick said. *You need only strike a kindred chord with one of them, and you're home free, son.*

Easy for the fucker to say. Kirkpatrick with his thousand-dollar suits, his fucking Jaguar. Snooty downstate way of talking made everybody else sound like their noses were stuffed. Looking at Fritz and his parents who were good decent Catholics like they were a bad smell in the room Kirkpatrick was too polite to acknowledge.

Now the Picks had jumped bail, everybody else's family was worried as hell they might try it, too. But Fritz had promised he would not no matter how desperate.

Since Fritz had been arrested, dragged into the NFPD van in handcuffs and roughed up at the precinct, he had not been himself. One of the cops had used a choke hold on him. Something had got ripped in his neck. His bowel problems dated to that night. Coming down from the meth high, his brain was fried. Couldn't sleep nights but during the day sometimes in his parents' house hearing Mom's TV. It was comforting, like being a little kid again and you've got a stomachache, earache, your mother lets you stay home from school. That night at the park, Fourth of July, the high school baseball tournament and there were teenage cheerleaders in satin costumes swinging their asses and titties. Frits wasn't sleeping but he would see these girls and groan aloud like one of them was grabbing his cock. Fritz had a thing for younger girls, his buddies teased him. A female over twenty was a turnoff, they knew too much and made actual wisecracks about the size of your cock. A young girl, really young like Maguire's daughter, is a different case. No wisecracks, she's gonna be scared as hell and respectful.

Fritz had to concede it was just as well probably Bethel Maguire had squirmed out of his grasp like a crazed eel. He'd have fucked the little bitch till she was dead meat. That kind of high, nothing can stop you. Like electricity charging through you. So now he'd be up for murder, he'd be really fucked.

Except if he'd killed the girl, or somebody'd killed her, and the mother, none of them would've been caught, maybe. No witnesses! Fritz Haaber wouldn't have been picked out of the police lineup by Bethel Maguire, wouldn't be in the shit he was in now breaking his mother's heart. *Your own fucking fault, see? You didn't act when you had the fucking chance.*

Now it was too late. The trial was starting. He could never get to the girl. He'd be watched, under surveillance. Sure he'd seen her a few times in the neighborhood, he'd parked across from the junior high to observe her departing, he'd followed her a little and she had not seen him, and at the mall the other day, just an accident he'd seen her there but he had followed her for a few minutes and it was fascinating watching her, this girl of maybe thirteen, not a pretty girl but sweet-faced, ashy-blond hair like the mother, walking with her grandma and the two of them wholly oblivious of being observed like with a telescope, almost Fritz came to think she could not see him he was invisible! A great feeling but fuck it she'd glanced up and seen him, and he liked it how scared she'd been, her face going dead white and looking like she was going to faint. Wild! A real rush! But Fritz knew, better get his ass out of there fast. Before the old-bag grandma sighted him, too, and started screaming.

He'd thought maybe some NFPD cops might come banging on his parents' door looking for him that night. Some crap about harassment of witnesses there was a law about. But no.

Bethel Maguire had not told. In her heart, Bethel Maguire had a thing for Fritz Haaber, huh?

Fritz was worried about this "forensics" shit. He knew it was real and all that, it was "hard science." He'd seen it on TV. Some kind of X-ray of semen, blood, hairs, clothes fibers. Like a jigsaw puzzle Kirkpatrick said these parts were, all of them scattered and the jurors were supposed to fit them back together to see if there should be a verdict of "guilty" or "not guilty." That was not so easy. You could distract and confuse the jurors, Kirkpatrick said. Because there is a wish in the heart of mankind to be distracted and confused. Truth is but one attraction, and not always the most powerful. Which was why Kirkpatrick insisted that his clients testify, and to memorize what Kirkpatrick had scripted for them. Already Kirkpatrick had led Fritz through his testimony so many times Fritz believed his brain was cracking. He was absolutely going nuts. No meth, not even dope, but he was allowed some beers. Needing to relax for Christ sake. He told Kirkpatrick he had not slept through a night nor had his bowels been normal in memory. He was lonely, too! His friends were keeping their distance for now. Even his relatives. And girls. They seemed scared of him, even girls who knew him from grade school. Even his girl cousins for Christ sake! It was insulting.

So when this call came, Fritz was primed for it.

A woman for him, saying it was urgent she speak to Fritz Haaber. Fritz took the call on the portable phone going off where his mother could not eavesdrop.

Afternoon of November 22. Three days before the trial. Christ he was nerved up! This female voice low and sexy in his ear saying she'd been seeing his picture on TV, in the papers. In the *Falls Clarion* the interview with Fritz's mom who sounded like the most wonderful supportive mother, that had made her cry almost. "That Woman Has Destroyed My Son's Life."

She knew some things about that Teena Maguire, her and her mother both knew plenty. She'd tell Fritz if he was interested. The kind of thing that should be aired in court, so the jury knew who this woman was. But mostly she just wanted to see Fritz. Her name was Louellen Drott. She'd transferred to Baltic High from Holy Redeemer and she'd graduated in 1993 she said. Fritz figured by this that she was three years behind him, he'd been class of '90 though he had not graduated. As the girl talked he was trying to recall Louellen Drott. The name Drott was a familiar name. There was a Drott Car Wash. There was a Drott who'd been a rookie for the Buffalo Bisons a few years back. Louellen said it was crucial that she see him that night. She had things to confide in him, and she had a rosary to give him. She knew from his photos that he was telling the truth about what had happened in the boathouse. He had warm sincere eyes that would not lie.

Louellen's voice was so sexy in his ear. Fritz shallowed hard. He knew that this was something special. It was like he was a wrongly condemned man, and Louellen was fated to save him. He could almost see her and he liked what he saw. She'd have long wavy hair possibly red-blond sliding over one eye. She'd be a petite girl. Fritz was five feet nine, he hated tall clunky girls who came on strong like lezzies. This Louellen Drott was not one of these.

In a lowered voice Louellen said there was this place where she worked, out by the airport, the Black Rooster Motel. She did not say exactly that she was a chambermaid at the motel but Fritz guessed this for she said she had access to all the rooms, and he could meet her in one. They would be "very private"—"no interruptions"—Louellen promised. The room at the farthest end of the motel was number 24 and she would be there waiting for him at 7:00 P.M., she would have DO NOT DISTURB hanging from the doorknob but he should just come inside, she'd be waiting.

Fritz said okay. His voice was weak asking should he bring a couple of six-packs? Or like maybe wine?

Louellen laughed saying no just bring yourself, Fritz. She would provide all that was needed, she promised!

Fritz felt close to swooning. Almost he could hear himself telling Marv Pick *Did I get laid last night! Man.*

Fritz shaved, and changed some of his clothes. Told his mom not to wait supper for him. Drove out the airport road. Fast-food restaurants and gas stations and industrial sites FOR LEASE and a strip of brightly lighted tacky motels at the end of which was the single-story cinder block BLACK ROOSTER. A neon sign flickered VAC NCIES. Fritz was so excited by this time, he'd been chewing the end of his cigarette. Fact was, nobody had been nice to him since the thing in July. Nobody gave a damn about Fritz really. Even before the thing in July. Donna had dumped him. None of her friends would go out with him. His mom gave her weepy interviews and prayed for him but he'd seen her stare at him sometimes, he knew that look of wonder and revulsion. Fritz's old man could not remain in the same proximity with Fritz for more than five minutes. His brothers and sister hated his guts. They were damn jealous, all the attention he was getting. All the money being pooled for his "defense." But Louellen Drott, she'd seen into Fritz's heart. She had a rosary for him. Before they fucked, they would say the rosary together. Or after they fucked. Or both. Louellen had been secretly in love with Fritz Haaber he guessed back at Baltic High. If Fritz got sent away to prison, Louellen would visit him. She would be faithful to him. The only fucking individual Fritz would consent to see and Louellen's picture too and interview would be printed in the *Clarion*.

When Fritz got paroled, they would be married. The 6:00 P.M. Fox TV News would do the interview.

*　　*　　*

It was off-season at Niagara Falls. Not many tourists this lousy time of year. Only a few rooms at the Black Rooster were occupied. These were nearest the highway, and farther from the airport runways. Fritz turned his car into the cinder lot and drove slowly to the end, where an outside light burned at number 24. Inside number 24 the interior was warmly lighted, the blind drawn. *She is waiting inside. Oh Christ.* Fritz counted just three vehicles parked outside the single-story motel. Two were parked by the manager's office and the third, a Ford station wagon, was parked in front of number 19.

Overhead, an airliner was just landing. Deafening screeching noise, made Fritz's teeth vibrate. It gave you a nervous rush like the first chords of heavy-metal rock. Breathless climbing out of the car pocketing his keys approaching the door where, sure enough, Do Not Disturb was hanging. "Louellen?" He turned the knob. The door was unlocked as she'd promised. His heart was beating so it hurt. In a hoarse hopeful voice he said, "Hello? Anybody here? This is Fritzie."

He'd love it for Louellen Drott to call him Fritzie. No one had called him Fritzie for a long time.

"Destroyed Son's Life"

T HE CHARRED AND UNRECOGNIZABLE corpse would be discovered in the late morning of November 23, 1996, at the end of a narrow access road a quarter mile from the Niagara Falls Airport, in a no-man's-land of underbrush and stunted trees. It would require no experienced medical examiner to determine that the body had been dosed with gasoline and set afire. An empty gallon can of gasoline was close by the corpse. A car was parked on the roadway, key in the ignition. Except for the car, identification of the corpse would have required some time. NFPD officers called in the license plate, and were informed that the vehicle was registered in the name of Fritz Haaber, 3392 Eleventh Street, Niagara Falls, New York.

Carefully placed on the car's dashboard ledge above the steering wheel was a handwritten note framed by a crystal rosary:

> God forgiv me and my family I am very ashamed. This will make things right   F. H.

The handwriting, though shaky, was identified as unmistakably that of left-handed Fritz Haaber. The rosary, the notepaper, the steering wheel of the car, the car door handles and interior, the gallon gasoline can: all were covered with Fritz Haaber's prints. On the ground close by the burned corpse was a book of matches from Arno's Fine Italian Foods & Pizzeria, which Fritz Haaber frequented, and this book of matches too was covered in Fritz Haaber's prints. It had been dropped some inches to the right of the body, approximately where it would have been dropped by a left-handed individual like Fritz Haaber holding the matchbook with his right hand and striking a match with his left.

Another time Gladys Haaber, the deceased young man's mother, would be interviewed for a cover story in the *Clarion*. Her grieving mother's portrait would appear beside a blown-up snapshot of her son Fritz taken several years before, in happier times when the boy was clean-shaven, no mustache and no straggly hair falling into his face and no jeering grin. It was never doubted by Gladys Haaber or by any of the Haabers that Fritz had taken his own young life in despair of being hounded by the Niagara County DA's office and that slut Teena Maguire for a crime he had not committed.

"My son was sensitive. He took things hard. He was driven to this. He could not sleep, he could not eat, and his bowels were never right anymore. Through the night we would hear the toilet flush. I hope they are happy now! These bloodsuckers who hide behind the law. I pray God that if there is justice on this earth it is exacted in the right place and on the right people, *soon.*"

Heaven

April 11, 1997
Dear Mom, & dear Bethie —
Its Heaven here! On the other side of
this card you see the "Joshua" cactus & the
blossoms are exactly like this. DeWitt & I
are so happy "on the road." The XL
Camper is something! You need 4-wheel
drive some of these sites. On these
camper parks you meet the damndest
characters but DeWitt can hold his
own. Bad weather at Esdras Park, flash
flood. Next is Grand Canyon. Met folks
from Buffalo & we all laughed at your
lousy weather back home, DeWitt is
the most generous decent man. I love
this new life with Gods grace. I think
of you there, God bless & keep my beloved
mother & daughter, Teena
(DeWitt SAYS HELLO!)

Mrs. Agnes Kovechi
& Bethel Maguire

2861 Baltic Ave.

Niagara Falls

N.Y.

14302

149

Part III

Lonely

From time to time you see him: Dromoor.

Always unexpectedly. Always it's a shock.

A young police officer in uniform. Climbing out of a police vehicle. Walking on the street. Once, in Central Park, on horseback riding with another officer. Lean, straight-backed, head close-shaven at the back and sides and dark glasses covering his eyes.

You pause, you're stricken into silence.

It's years later. It's another world. This world of urban New York City where you and your husband live, in no way contiguous with the lost world of your Niagara Falls girl-hood. As your husband is in no way kindred to the boys and men you'd known in that world, of whom you have told him virtually nothing.

When will you tell him? Maybe never. For why tell him? He would not understand. There was ugliness in that world but there was beauty, too. There was hatred, but love. Only one man could understand and your husband is not that man.

You know that Dromoor isn't a uniformed police officer any longer. He isn't assigned to the street. He's Detective

First Class John Dromoor, he wears clothes like any civilian coat, probably a white shirt, a tie. Not likely he'd be in New York City, either. Last you heard he was still with the NFPD promoted and transferred to the First Precinct.

Last you heard was years ago. Before even your mother married her friend DeWitt. Ex-navy man she'd met at the Christian Fellowship Tabernacle where a woman friend from AA had taken her.

A long time ago. After Fritz Haaber. After the surviving rapists plea-bargained degrees of guilt, accepted prison sentences and agreed to no trial.

No trial. Teena burst into tears, so grateful.

You have to concede, by now Dromoor would be middle-aged. Hard to imagine that man other than he'd been but in fact it's possible you wouldn't recognize him.

"Beth? Is something wrong?"

Your husband is touching your arm. Sometimes he's annoyed by these sudden fugues of yours on the street, sometimes he's concerned. He never seems to see who, or what has captivated your attention so that you stand transfixed staring. And then, waking from the trance, you feel a wave of heat rising into your face as if you've been slapped. You stammer, "Why—why do you ask?"

"You looked so lonely, suddenly. As if you'd forgotten I'm here."